# L(

# From

# Darkness

## Keith R. Baker

Keith R. Baker/K and L Products Press
P.O. Box 114
Ronan, Montana, USA/59864
www.KeithRBaker.com

Publisher's Note: This is a work of fiction. Names, characters, places, and
incidents are a product of the author's imagination. Locales and public
names are sometimes used for atmospheric purposes. Any resemblance to
actual people, living or dead, or to businesses, companies, events,
institutions, etc. is completely coincidental.

LONGSHOT FROM DARKNESS/ Keith R. Baker -- 1st ed.
ISBN:1542382327
ISBN-13: 978-1542382328

# DEDICATION

Dedicated to all those who would like to know what really happened, even though we were not present during the historic events preceding out lives., and especially those who recognize that most accounts handed down to us were devised by those with incredible agendas and even appetites. We may never find the truth completely, but at least may we always question that which has been taught to us by and for the convenience of others.

Question everything and everyone!

Keith R. Baker

# CONTENTS

# ACKNOWLEDGMENTS

To each and all those who helped this writer in whatever ways to bring for this work of fiction as an exploration of possible truth. You and I both know who you are, and I, for one, thank you all dearly This applies most of all to those loyal readers who encourage the efforts.

# CHAPTER ONE

# Overlooking

*Friday, July 3, 1863. Some minutes past two o'clock in the afternoon, a hundred and more yards east of the Emmitsburg Road, Gettysburg, Pennsylvania.*

Patrick lurched to his right in reaction to the nearby whistling of a miniè ball passing his left ear. What those specially designed bullets could do to a human body terrified him. He had been lightly grazed by one just two days earlier, during the opening day of this tremendous battle. The resulting gash on the outside of his left thigh was bad enough. Though well-bandaged against re-opening the wound, the pain throbbing from where the heavy bullet passed was plenty to remind him of the mortal danger they all faced.

Corporal Patrick Murphy continued his march toward the low stone wall ahead. Since crossing the rail fence, they were veering more to the left than previously. He suspected the regiment would soon break into the running charge of final assault. Scattered outbursts of their Rebel yell could be heard on his left and on his right. Those came from men trying to steady themselves and perhaps rally their comrades.

Sweat poured down his forehead; it also flowed freely under his woolen tunic. He imagined the dark stain of it growing across the back of his 8th Virginia Volunteer Infantry uniform. Another miniè sizzled past, again close to his left ear. This time, his involuntary flinch caused him to stumble. As he twisted to regain his balance, he caught sight of the red mist exploding from the head of a man in the rank behind him. A man whom he didn't know, now dead on his feet–the corpse dropping to the ground. The miniè ball that had so closely missed Patrick's own head had found its mark in the head of this other.

His fear made him sick, as did the sight. Despite not knowing the dead man and despite already seeing so much carnage in this war, his gorge started to rise. Patrick fought against the rising burn of vomit in his throat–the taste of it in his mouth. He could not let the men see him retch. Especially not now, when they were so close and after so many had already died in this hell called Gettysburg. As their corporal, he had to keep going forward, leading from the front. He swallowed hard while telling his legs to keep stepping to the cadence.

Ten yards to his right and perhaps ten feet ahead of him was the officer Patrick was guiding on, Lieutenant William Leslie. Like himself, the lieutenant had been promoted just this morning. The regiment had suffered heavy losses in the battles leading up to this one. Newly-promoted non-coms and officers had become an all-to-common occurrence for the men to have much reaction any longer.

Stepping off at two o'clock in the afternoon for this frontal attack against the Union lines meant that the troops would be fighting not only enemy soldiers before them but the worst heat of the day as well. The hot, sticky humidity of this Pennsylvania summer day made the difficult task of charging enemy lines that much harder.

The remaining men of the 8th Virginia had their rifles loaded, moving forward with the bayonets fixed. Each man would have one shot to offer against the blue line ahead; after that they could expect to charge pell-mell into the fray of hand-to-hand combat, using their bayonets to skewer and fight those arrayed against them. Reloading would not be an option for the Confederates reaching and breeching the wall.

As they continued to wheel left, climbing the slight incline leading to their objective, Patrick was again grateful to have the lieutenant out ahead of him. Each time a wave of fear sent a shiver through his body he was tempted to drop to the ground and remain hidden by the tall grass. But with each such temptation he forced himself to glance at Leslie. Lieutenant William Leslie, carrying his sword in his left hand and a revolver in his right, striding straight into volley after volley of the Union rifles aimed at him. The man must have nerves of iron to walk so tall and proud amidst the thunderous noise and chaos surrounding him.

At that moment, the lieutenant spun around to face his men while continuing to march backwards, all the while keeping his pace steady. Leslie raised his sword and shouted in his gentle Virginia drawl, "By the half-quick, men. Let's send 'em t' hell where they belong." His voice could barely be heard above the din of battle. As he turned back round to again face the enemy, the lieutenant let out his version of the high-pitched Rebel battle cry. Patrick and the others picked up the cry which grew in volume as it carried forward. Other Confederate units in this massive attack also picked up the cry. Soon the entire field of battle was swept by the eerie, unsettling sound.

Breaking into a run to match that of his lieutenant, Murphy realized they were now heading directly for the copse of trees, just as they had been briefed to do. He thought for a few moments about the fact that the regiment was perfectly aligned to attack their assigned objective. This after skirting around and stepping over countless bodies of horses and men strewn about the field from the previous day's fighting. The odors were beyond description.

A concussive boom of Union cannon firing from the right refocused his attention. At this short range they would be using canister rounds to cut down as many charging Rebels as possible with each shot. Sure enough, the whistling sound, like an entire nest of attacking hornets, filled the air then passed. But that passing extracted a painful toll from the 8th Virginia.

Lieutenant Leslie was nowhere to be seen, and the number of men left, right, and behind was reduced by about half. The realization that he might now be the highest ranking member of his unit clutched at his resolve, he felt weak in his knees–even feared he might collapse. A surge of renewed determination gave him a burst of energy, and perhaps courage, to drive himself and his men forward.

Then all of a sudden he was there. Past the wall and surrounded by Yanks and his own comrades, all of them locked in mortal combat. The rifles had been fired and the bayonets were stabbing and jabbing forward, though without great effect. Some men on both sides had taken to swinging rifles as clubs. The butt end of one such swinging rifle collided with Murphy's head, knocking him to the ground.

While he lay there watching the blue sky blurring above him, Patrick Murphy wondered if he ever would again see his sister. Would he ever meet the man who had married her? A man named Rob Finn, a sergeant in the Union Army from Wisconsin. Would they meet here, on the field of battle? And what of Bridget herself? He'd not had a letter from her for more than eighteen months. These thoughts wandered through his mind behind dazed eyes as he remained motionless, pain creeping throughout his body.

Patrick's view of the sky dimmed as he pondered his next-of-kin and her fate. Strange that both of them had emigrated from Ireland, Bridget to settle in Wisconsin, and he in Virginia. They were much nearer one another now than they had been in the years before he crossed the ocean to this new land. He had stepped off the ship and into this insane war! His vision dimmed again before he blacked out.

As for his older sister, Bridget Murphy Riley Finn, Patrick never received notification that cholera carried her away the previous year, in April of 1862. His brother-in-law, Rob, whom he'd never met, did not send a letter. Rob knew of Patrick, but not of his whereabouts. And as for meeting Rob in opposition on the field of battle, Patrick need not have worried. At that moment, Rob Finn was more than 2,000 miles away in the gold fields of the Idaho Territory.

\* \* \*

*Friday, July 3, 1863. Mid-afternoon, on the hill north of the town of Bannack, Idaho Territory.*

Rob and Lonnie exchanged looks of surprise and amazement after gazing out across the small valley before them. Lonnie remarked, "These folks sure have been busy since we left. Surely they have." The horses, Bricks and Roxie, nodded their heads as if agreeing with their riders.

Horses and riders were all anxious enough to get into town and end the day's trek.

The bustling scene below and the warm clear day again reminded Rob that it had been only six months since their last visit to Bannack. It had been much colder then, and now the growing city's appearance was different to the eye.

When Finn and Walters left Bannack last December there were no plans for them to return this soon, if at all. At that time, plans had been put into place to acquire gold directly from the miners and assure that the gold shipments would reach their intended destinations in Salt Lake City and Denver. There were two Treasury Department agents in place and Rob had hired Henry Plummer to look after the Pinkerton Agency's interests in the district. Those plans and the men in place seemed satisfactory when Rob and Lonnie left for Salt Lake City.

The growth and expansion of the town were obvious in that first glance–it amazed the eye to take in the sheer amount of work that had been done. There were more than double the number of buildings and tents from when they'd left. The Goodrich Hotel, in which they intended to board while here, was no longer in Yankee Flat. It had been moved to the north side of the main street in the growing city, as had Cyrus Skinner's Saloon.

Then in May, another gold strike had been made less than seventy miles from Bannack, one which many thought would be the largest find of placer gold yet. That new strike was drawing prospectors from around the country, including more than a few from Bannack. The mining camps springing up in Alder Gulch were reported to be expanding faster than had those of Bannack the prior year.

The people of the United States, and their government, were hungry for gold as never before. The same was true for the people and government of the Confederate States. Though uniforms were not evident in the gold fields, competition between the factions was present. Tension could be felt everywhere one went; gunfights were common.

Henry Plummer, the elected sheriff for the Bannack mining district and secret contract service provider to the Pinkerton Agency, had been reporting troubling activities and developments to Rob ever since he and Lonnie had left. Thefts and robberies were becoming so frequent that the amount of gold arriving at the mints had slowed to almost nothing. The governments, both North and South, were desperate for gold with which to fund their war efforts.

These were the elements contributing to Rob and Lonnie being ordered back into the gold country at this time. His orders came from Abraham Lincoln thru Allan Pinkerton. Rob wondered how many operatives had been sent by the Confederates, imagining the number could already be considerable.

Adding to concern about Confederate agents operating in the vicinity was the fact that the political division among the prospectors was significant. Rob and Lonnie took some comfort in the knowledge that Henry Plummer was on their side in this undeclared conflict. Plummer supported the Union cause in this war between the states.

*  *  *

There were things to be done as they settled into Bannack, before their investigative work could go forward. Prior to putting any plans or actions into effect, they needed to meet with Plummer and to re-establish themselves as the holders of the mining claim they had purchased the preceding December. A miner by the name of McNally had been hired at that time to work the claim, thus keeping it under their ownership. McNally had been directed to report to the two US Treasury Department agents and to Plummer regarding his finds and production. That output had been slim. While Plummer had not accused McNally of pocketing gold from the claim, his reports left no doubt that he considered it a possibility.

Among the difficulties in the business of gold mining in western districts was that of finding reliable men to do the work for wages and turn over all of the precious metal found to their employers. Glittering yellow metal had a strong pull on even those who were normally honest.

With no other eyes watching, it was a simple matter to transfer portions of a day's find to their own purse rather than that of their employer or partners. This fact also contributed to the number of violent altercations taking place almost daily in the mining districts.

From their overlook of the town they had seen that the "diggings", where the gold actually came out of the ground, had about tripled in the months they were away. Their own claim, which belonged to the Pinkerton Agency, was near to where the mining activity was greatest.

\* \* \*

Rob was thinking over events from home which took place before he left for this assignment. When the time to leave arrived, some things in their new home town of Delavan were unsettled. Most pressing of these matters in the Finn household was the conflict between his new bride, Maggie, and his two oldest children, Catherine and John.

Catherine was out of the house now, living in an apartment in Chicago with her infant son, Thomas (named after his father and grandfather). Things between Catherine and Maggie were such that they no longer spoke to one another.

Catherine was fourteen years old and already a widow and mother. Rob's income from the Pinkerton Agency was such that he could help her with finances, when she would allow such help. Though young, she was strong and independent. She had been taking in laundry for others; she also baked meat-and-vegetable Irish pasties which she sold to a small restaurant around the corner from her apartment. She was making ends meet.

When her baby, Thomas Duffy III, arrived in June, Rob was relieved that mother and baby were both well. Catherine accepted his financial help then, but with her insisting it would end as soon as she was able to return to her normal routine. He found he was quite proud that she was so self-sufficient.

John had been struggling, not only at his new stepmother constantly correcting his language, but also because she assigned him so many household chores that he felt he was neglecting his farm chores. And he had almost no time he could call his own–time which Rob knew John would be spending with his friends at the Mabie Brothers Circus encampment. The circus owned several hundred acres just north and east of the Finn family property. The Mabie's land fronted on Delavan Lake. The circus also owned two elephants which drew John's attention like a pair of giant magnets.

John was ten years old this year, big for his age and already developing a mind of his own. John was also well aware of the situation that existed between Catherine and Maggie. He envied Catherine that she was out from under Maggie's frequent scolding and nagging.

Rob recognized the resentment in his son and had tried to calm the relationship between John and Maggie. They both behaved well enough toward one another after his "sit-down" talk with them before he departed for the territories. He suspected the peace was a temporary show in response to his request that they "get along as natural family."

Rob's assignment might keep him away from home for several months, perhaps longer. In marrying Maggie McDonald one year after his children's mother, Bridget, had died, he was fulfilling an obligation to her. He needed a wife to care for the home and the younger children, which Maggie was willing enough to do. His conscience bothered him that his was a marriage of convenience; that he felt no particular romantic attraction for his new wife. But Maggie wanted to be married and let it be known that Rob was her intended, so that was that.

On the day Rob left, Maggie had informed him that she believed she was "in a family way". That happy fact was the result of Rob's keen sense of duty to give his young bride the children she wanted. He was still unable to overlook Maggie's heavy-handedness in dealing with Catherine and the other children. Now he was beginning to worry she might also drive John away from home with her sharp tongue and demanding nature. And the circus was always looking for help in the traveling crew.

\* \* \*

A small blast from across the valley surprised Bricks. The big horse shifted his weight, and Rob was right back into the moment. He could see the smoke from the blasting powder rising on the still air and hear the ore being shoveled to where it could be washed. There are all kinds of overlooks in this life, he reflected, some much easier to experience than others.

While Rob and Lonnie rode their horses slowly downslope toward the main street of Bannack, their movements were watched by a shady-looking threesome, also mounted, with their hats pulled down hiding their faces. Rob and Lonnie had seen them across the valley before starting their descent into the Grasshopper diggings.

"Those fellas seem mighty interested in us, Rob. Suppose that's the new Bannack welcoming committee?" Lonnie's suggestion was less than sincere.

"We'll hope it's just their healthy interest in lookin' out for their own claim or some such. We certainly don't want any special attention just now."

They were able to secure a room in Goodrich's establishment without difficulty, though the daily rate had almost doubled since their last stay. No doubt the prices for meals would also have increased, as had everything else in the growing town.

Goodrich himself checked them in and, recognizing them from their previous stay, was friendly in his demeanor.

As was their habit when working together on assignment, Rob and Lonnie shared a room. The hotel now boasted wooden floors throughout, an improvement from the last time they'd stayed. They again had a ground-floor room, much to their liking.

It was yet early enough that they had plenty of time for dinner, (Goodrich having assured them he wouldn't close the kitchen until later), so they decided to look for Henry Plummer to invite as a dining companion. Rob figured they had a lot of catching up to do. He and Lonnie finished arranging things in their room and were just heading to the door when they heard the sharp rap of knuckles on wood. Rob opened the door to find Henry Plummer wearing his brace of pistols and a large smile, standing just outside.

# CHAPTER TWO

# News From Below

*Saturday, July 4, 1863. Breakfast in the dining room of the Goodrich Hotel, Bannack, Idaho Territory.*

It had taken the threesome several hours to complete dinner the evening before, during which they sat at the same table that they now occupied. Tucked into a corner, this table position allowed them to keep their backs to the walls and observe all foot traffic in the dining room while they discussed their private business matters in low voice.

"Let me see if Ah've got this right. Yer sayin' that the robberies are bein' carried out by members of the Knights of the Golden Circle, but the local Masons won't turn 'em in because they're part of the same club?" Rob's tone reflected his incredulity toward the matter.

"Not exactly part of the *same* fraternity, but that's the gist of it." Plummer paused to sip his coffee and give his companions an opportunity to question further his report from the previous evening.

Lonnie Walters, Rob's partner on this mission, had been almost silent during their dinner together, and other than his morning greeting, hadn't said a word during breakfast. He now asked Plummer simply, "But if the

Masons are Union supporters, 'n' the Knights are Rebel supporters, why wouldn't they turn 'em in?"

"Beats me. I've been tryin' to figure what's going on with these fellas. Even tried to join the Masons ... couple o' times. They won't have anything to do with me. Maybe I've been blackballed or something like that. And it's been that way since before we all went to Salt Lake City last winter. I don't know what they were thinking about me before, but since I've been elected Sheriff, they're really keeping their distance. And it may not matter, since I'm not sure who is behind the robberies. There's still too many possibilities to consider." Plummer's frustration with the situation was obvious to the other two.

"What have Emry an' Daniels done t' help your investigations, Henry?" Rob questioned after considering what had just been discussed.

"Those two? They've done nothing. They're never around until just after the action is over. Don't think I don't have doubts about those two."

Plummer finished his comment just in time to see Ned McNally approaching their table, hat in hand, and looking sheepishly around at the three already seated there.

"Come along an' join us, McNally. Have ya had yer breakfast yet?" Rob's welcome was genuine and effusive as always.

McNally waved aside the offer for breakfast, but accepted coffee from Goodrich when he arrived with a mugful of the stuff. His clothes were the rough canvas trousers preferred by miners, held in place by a set of wide suspenders. Covering his well-muscled upper body was a sweat-stained, close-fitting cotton shirt open at the throat. His boots had bits of drying mud still clinging aboard, and a fine coating of fresh dust covered his outfit, and the man, completely. Small streaks of mud marked his long face where drops of sweat had left tracks. As he sat down and fidgeted with his hat, tiny clouds of dust arose from off his various parts. McNally seemed oblivious to any of this.

The others waited politely for the newcomer to finish several swallows of hot coffee as they looked toward him, expectantly. Finally, after what seemed to Rob a reasonable time, he asked, "What news of our diggin's can ya give us, McNally? Is our claim startin' t' pay off?"

At his best, the term slow-and-steady was an accurate description of the miner. Rob and Lonnie had been aware of this trait when they'd hired him to work the claim. McNally didn't have resources enough to buy his own claim, and the flurry of staking and claiming following the initial finds in Bannack had quickly closed off the opportunity to those arriving only a few weeks later. Ned McNally applied for the position when they posted it with George Crisman the preceding December. After an interview and period of working with the man at that time, they had found him reliable and trustworthy enough to work the claim in their absence. After all, Henry Plummer and the two Treasury Department agents would be on location to keep an eye on him.

"I've had some good day's finds comin' outta that claim, sirs, but nothin' like this before!" His voice rose to a crescendo as his fist slammed down on the table, where he opened it leaving a bulging leather poke and four gold nuggets, each nugget the size of a pistol ball. McNally's smile revealed a couple of missing teeth, but his joy was sincere in sharing what he knew to be good news with his employers.

Rob placed an extended index finger before his own mouth as he smoothly placed his napkin over the objects on the table that McNally had just set there. His signal and intentions were obvious, but he added, "Let's keep our voices down an' this news t' ourselves, gentlemen, shall we?"

"Oh! Sorry!" McNally's voice was now hushed. "I got so excited, I kinda forgot myself. All this come up just this mornin'. Usually I report my big finds to Mr. Emry, but he told me yesterday mornin' not to expect to see him for awhile. Said he had some business to attend to up North." He looked embarrassed.

"Not t' worry, not t' worry. There's no one about, just now." Rob's tone and demeanor were calming. "Did Emry happen t' mention where in the North his business might take him?"

"Just said he had a lot of traveling to do and rivers to cross. Didn't say exactly when he'd be back, but I got the idea it wouldn't be soon."

"Thanks, Ned. That's good t' know. Have ya seen Daniels lately?" Rob's eyebrows rose slightly when he posed this last question.

"Emry says Daniels spends all his time at the new diggin's in Alder Gulch, Mr. Finn. I hardly ever see him at all, and it's been a while since the last time. That last time I saw him an' Emry together they were arguin' somethin' fierce. Neither ever told me what that was about, and I didn't ask. They were both angry. Red-faced, if ya know what I mean."

"I do indeed, Ned. Thank ya again. Why don't ya take a little rest an' I'll stop by t' see ya this afternoon. Maybe after the parade, if ya wouldn't mind? Henry knows where yer livin', does he not?"

McNally nodded in the affirmative and rose from his seat. Looking sheepishly around again, he turned and left the building.

After the outer door closed behind the man, Rob looked back to his remaining companions. "Ah suspect that he is far more honest than most, an' what bothers me is that this is the first of any finds that I'm hearin' of. Nothing has come t' me from the Treasury Department nor other channels. Henry?"

"News to me, Rob. Emry always says that our claim is a waste of time and Treasury Department money. But he speaks well of McNally. Seems to like the chap. I haven't seen Daniels in a while, but he never talks to me even when he is around, and won't look me in the eye. I've been thinkin' that McNally must be pocketing most of what he finds on the claim, but now I'm inclined to agree with you–McNally's not the thief in our midst." Plummer's face clouded over with a mixture of embarrassment and anger.

"It does make me wonder, too, Henry. Ah may have an idea of what's going on here, but right now it's just a hunch." Rob looked equally puzzled.

$$* * *$$

After leaving the hotel Rob stopped in at George Crisman's store for a visit. He needed to continue gathering information about local events that occurred during his months back in the States, and Crisman was as reliable a source as any in Bannack. After satisfying himself about several details, Rob decided to take a hike up the hill north of the town, generally parallel to the wagon trail to Alder Gulch. He found a stony perch above the diggings of some claims.

He chose to sit a while and ponder the activities of mining districts. Lots of men were hard at work digging the soils or gravels into conveyances to be hauled and washed. What made one claim payoff, while those adjoining it were barren? Lonnie had gone to check on their stabled horses and then see if he could locate Daniels or information regarding where he or Emry might be headed.

Wondering about the latest developments with the Pinkerton claim in Bannack, Rob recalled details from their dinner and breakfast discussions, together with other facts and happenings. Much had happened in this mining district while he and Lonnie had been away. Many of his mental exercises had to do with the two Treasury Department agents. He knew them to be employed by the Treasury Department and had run background investigations on both when he'd been in Chicago and St. Louis verifying that fact. Emry had some experience in banking and Daniels had been a teamster before becoming a clerk in the Chicago office of the Treasury Department branch there. Nothing amiss about either of their pasts from those sources .

Rob considered information about Henry Plummer's activities which had come from the man himself, together with what he had learned of him last December, and from other sources since. He took into account reports Plummer had telegraphed to the Chicago office and a few reports that'd been in the news where Plummer was mentioned. Crisman's comments all matched what Plummer had been saying.

He mulled over the actions in which Henry had been involved. Henry had explained the shooting that led to Jack Cleveland's death. Those details also matched what George Crisman had shared. And there'd been plenty of witnesses when Cleveland verbally challenged and drew his pistol against Plummer. Those witnesses present in Skinner's Saloon had all said the same thing.

Plummer had gone on to explain that Cleveland had been obsessed with Electa Bryan, Plummer's fiancèe, and that Cleveland had threatened Henry more than once. Cleveland had even gone so far as to plant a rumor with the thenBannack sheriff, Hank Crawford, that Plummer was responsible for the death a lawman in California and that he, Plummer, was planning to ambush Crawford. Sadly, Crawford believed Cleveland's story and, though not present himself, was further convinced of Cleveland's story by the shootout between Cleveland and Plummer. Acting on this belief, Crawford ambushed Henry Plummer, hitting him in the right forearm with a rifle shot from across a street.

The outcome of that episode was that Crawford packed up and left the territory that night, never to return. Plummer's wound caused him to lean heavily on his left hand for nearly everything, including gun play. His right arm had been in a sling for a couple of months and Henry was convinced it would never heal completely to its former usefulness.

As part of his regular contract duties for the Pinkerton agency, Henry had been steadily arranging for gold shipments to leave the town and travel south to Salt Lake City on the way to Denver. Plenty of merchants, miners and others vouched that Plummer had taken pains to handle details quietly and with reputable teamsters. No one was suggesting that Plummer was anything other than honest and diligent in trying to solve the string of robberies.

Regarding specific details of gold shipment and supply train robberies, two groups of culprits were most often mentioned. The first of these gangs had been reported to be local groups of Bannock or Shoshone Indians. Robberies by Indians stopped immediately after the Bear River Massacre by the US Army at the end of January. Then, a few weeks later, Indians were again being named among those attacking the gold shipments. The recent descriptions of these Indians did not match those of the earlier attackers. This led Rob to wonder if a different tribe or tribes had become involved, or if the robbers were truly Indians at all. It would be easy enough for criminals to disguise themselves as Indians to divert attention from their own identities.

The other group of outlaws committing robberies in the gold district were of the road agent type. With bandanas covering their faces, a mounted group of these men, armed with rifles or shotguns, would block the route of the travelers. Then one would come forward and, disguising his voice, make the demands for the group. Details from survivors were not consistent and not necessarily reliable. Robberies committed by this type also were on the rise. Added to the growing number of incidents was the fact that the road agent gangs and Indian bands often left their victims dead or wounded. Fear spread among the miners, gold dealers and general populace, so that a clamor arose for an active and capable lawman in the district. By the end of February, gold leaving from and supply cargoes arriving in Bannack had again slowed to a trickle. It was this string of events that led to Plummer being elected sheriff in March.

Then, in April, there had been an unprovoked incident in which a man named Buck Stinson shot and killed Chief Snag and at least one other Indian. More shooting erupted and several other Indians were killed and wounded. Stinson was an occasional deputy of Plummer's, and the investigation did not clearly resolve what started the violence, thus no further action was taken. Cyrus Skinner proudly displayed several Indian scalps in his saloon afterward until Plummer convinced him to take them down.

Following all of this, there was the new gold strike in Alder Gulch in May. Henry Plummer's marriage with Electa Bryan in Sun River took place a mere two weeks before Rob and Lonnie arrived in Bannack. The newlyweds had only just settled into Henry's cabin in the mining town.

Lonnie's mellow, calm voice startled Rob, he had been so lost in his thoughts. "Roxie an' Bricks 're both doing fine, Rob. Plenty o' fresh water an' hay. Enough oats to kept their weight on, not enough to make 'em feisty. They're well-stabled and well-cared for, this trip." His mahogany features showed a smile broad with satisfaction at being able to deliver such an encouraging report about their horses. Both men had firm attachments to their mounts.

"So glad to hear that news, Lonnie. Have a seat an' join me. Thought we might think and visit for a bit. Maybe wait here for the parade to start." Rob motioned to a level spot alongside himself where Lonnie could sit.

The two Pinkerton detective partners had a great deal of trust and respect for one another. Each had helped the other to survive on more than one occasion. Theirs was a friendship born of experience, integrity, and mutual goals. They conversed in low tones for about an hour before the first strains of the brass instruments tuning up reached their ears. After standing and brushing the dust from their trousers, they walked most of the way down the hill. From the place they stopped they would be able to view the small, but energetic company of participants in the Fourth of July celebration. They could also keep watch on the comings and goings of the threesome watching from a corresponding perch across the gulch. They were the same three who had been watching the Pinkertons' arrival the previous day.

* * *

*Sunday, July 5, 1863. The Finn family farm south and east of Delavan, Wisconsin.*

John Finn, though only ten years old, had had enough. The screen door banged shut behind him as he continued his hurried exit off the property. His feet only touched the porch and the stairs once each in his run to escape his nemesis, the woman he was required to call stepmother. For his tender age, he understood much more than the adults in his life gave him credit for.

He knew his father had married Maggie to take care of the younger children because he could not be home with them all the time. He understood why his father had insisted John call her stepmother. He also understood that his father would never approve of the way Maggie ordered him around nor her being bossy with the younger kids. Mary was not yet eight and Robert, Jr. was only four. They could still get used to having this twenty-year-old bring them up. But John was just plain fed up–done.

As he reached the tree-line behind the big barn he heard Maggie bellow, "You come back here, John Finn, and right this instant if you know what's good for you." He didn't even break stride knowing there was no way she could catch him and she wouldn't even try. He was through the trees and following northeastward along the edge of the swamp in no time. He soon reached the lakeshore and followed it to the Mabie Brothers Circus encampment. He had already made his mind up to join this circus as an animal handler. He hoped they would take him on for the job. He further hoped they would be leaving the area again soon.

We all would do well to be cautious of the things we hope for.

* * *

*Saturday, July 18, 1863. Near the top of the slope overlooking the town of Bannack from the north.*

Rob's long stride covered the uphill climb quickly, but he had been so preoccupied with his thoughts about the goings on that he didn't even notice John Wilson until he had almost reached the outcropping on which Wilson stood.

"Howdy, Rob. It's been awhile. Heard you were back in the district," Wilson's easy greeting reminded Rob of the help he'd received from this man during the past December. Not only was he a reliable and capable messenger, he had acted as scout and guide when Rob and Lonnie needed to reach Salt Lake City.

"Six months and more already, John. I wasn't expectin' to find you up here." Rob paused to catch his breath, surprised to find how out of breath he'd become climbing such a short while. Being at these higher altitudes took some getting used to, he recalled to himself. After puffing another few moments, he added, "How've ya been?"

"Mostly good, I'd say. Still got my scalp and haven't lost any horses. Mighty glad to be done troopin' these days, though. All this gold minin' has got everything and everyone stirred up. And that Bear River outing was a real nasty business."

"Oh? Is that so?" Rob was eager to hear another perspective on that military action. The only reports he'd seen described it as a total success in which the Army had carried out its orders to the letter.

"You know, I just missed bein' there myself. I was headed back up to Bannack with them two Treasury fellas after we left you in Salt Lake City. I've always preferred the western route along Weston Creek, even though it runs to a higher altitude. It keeps me and my traffic from disturbin' the Shoshone villages in the valley more so than the Montana trail. Besides, I'm always on horseback and don't need a wagon track.

"I had a lot of friends among the Shoshone. That was before the massacre, of course. We always got along well, and traded fairly back and forth. Even had four among them agree to watch after my shacks and spare horses. They were neighborly and trustworthy–which is more than I can say for some of my white acquaintances.

"Then, all that trouble between the Indians and the settlers last summer and fall came up. A number of the

Mormon farmers in the valley felt that the Indians had been unfairly provoked by a hangin' last summer that should never have happened. In the beginnin' of December, an Army firing squad executed four Shoshone braves captured after a skirmish. Details don't match the stories. Chief Bear Hunter's band had plenty of reasons to be stirred up. Colonel Connor's troops got involved after some judge issued warrants for the chiefs of the tribe to be arrested and brought in for questioning. It may be that the Colonel had another idea about how to handle the disagreement; I wouldn't know. I was trying to avoid the Cache Valley, like I always do. Thought it even more important with all the recent trouble. Then the weather turned against us.

"Anyhow, there'd been a lot of snowfall in the high country since you an' Lonnie an' I passed that way a couple weeks before, so we had to turn back not long after leaving the valley. Went back south as far as Ogden and spent over a week there. Then the weather broke a little; there was even a thaw startin' when we set out the second time. We re-supplied and started north again. And things seemed to be goin' pretty well, at first.

"Reachin' the high trail wasn't too bad and walkin' was pretty good until the second day we were on it. Up there, the snow hadn't melted down as much. We weren't makin' good time at all–snow was just too deep and lots of icy places. The horses were worn out so we had to take turns walkin' lead to break trail just to keep goin'. Me an'

Daniels did, anyways. Emry said he couldn't take a turn at breakin' trail, him being so short, ya know.

"Then, when we were about played out, we reached my line shack on a shoulder of Old Mount Baldy. Decided to rest up for a day or so. It was lucky for us we did. A big blizzard came onto the west side of that mountain; forced us to hole up for two weeks. It got so cold we brought the horses inside. Their heat helped keep us all alive. There was only a bit of flour and small sack of dried beans in the cabin. We got plenty hungry, Rob, waitin' for that storm to move on. Pine cones an' needles an' bark don't fill a belly—man nor horse. Finally it was hunger drove us out of the shack.

"We hadn't planned to come off down the east side, but, like I said, we were mighty hungry an' the horses were worse off than we were. I was hopin' to get help from my Shoshone friends when we got down to their village on Battle Creek. It was colder than I ever remember; I was afraid we might not make it. Bein' as we were all on what you might call our last legs, we were movin' mighty slow. We didn't camp on the way down. Just built fires to warm ourselves an' melt snow to drink. Didn't make more than a couple miles a day movin' like that. By the time we got down into the valley we were hardly movin' at all; must've looked like ghosts shufflin' along. I was at the absolute end of my rope, certain I couldn't take another step when we saw smoke in the distance. Emry stopped an' refused to go any further. He wanted us go on ahead an' send someone to fetch him into the village. What Daniels an' I found when we got to the Shoshone encampment caused us to step more lively.

"I've seen a lot of battlefields during my time in the cavalry, Rob, but I've never seen anything like that. There were dead Indians everywhere, and I do mean everywhere: men, women, children. I read in the Deseret News edition a week later that between 250 and 300 Indians were killed. Well, I can tell you the number of dead Shoshone was a lot higher than that. Some of the bodies were in big piles together; others scattered around in smaller bunches and a lot them alone or in twos or threes. Most of 'em shot at close range–the powder burns on their frozen skin were plain to see. That whole action was a disgrace to the U.S. Army and all those in government that let it happen.

"My friend, Chief Sagwitch, somehow survived. We ended up helpin' each other. Daniels an' I helped the Indians with their dead an' wounded; the Shoshones shared their winter stores with us–enough for us to continue on North. Emry was his usual useless self. Didn't lift a finger to help with the work, he stayed by the fire keepin' himself warm addin' wood he didn't even help gather. Oh, an' he ordered Daniels an' me around like we were his servants. Not that I followed his orders.

"There wasn't much help we could give to the Indians, so we left when we got our strength back an' after doin' what we could–I think that was on the fourth day. Travel after that was better because there was less snow, but it was still mighty cold. It took us ten days of steady marchin' and ridin' to finally reach Bannack. We were in pretty sorry shape when we got here. Daniels lost of couple of toes to frostbite. One of the Treasury horses had to be destroyed; no savin' that one. Townsfolk appreciated the meat, though. Food had been plenty scarce in Bannack that month, what with no supplies comin' in and no buffalo meat." Wilson shook his head as if clearing a bad vision.

The way Wilson ended his story, Rob was certain there would be no more details forthcoming. Then Wilson asked, "What brings you back to the gold district, if you don't mind my askin'? I thought you'd gone back to the States for good."

"The robberies of gold shipments has the Federal government worried. The North an' the South are both tryin' t' get their hands on as much of the stuff as they can. And neither wants the other t' get any of it. I'm pokin' around t' see what we can turn up." Rob trusted Wilson, who already knew of his Pinkerton connection and who supported the Union cause, at least tacitly so. "Ya wouldn't happen to have any ideas about who's behind these robberies, would ya, John?" There was no accusation in Rob's question. He was merely seeking information from a man he believed to be reliable and honest.

"You might recall that I have had reasons to be suspicious of those Treasury men from the start, especially with them followin' me around the territory before we knew who they were. My feelings have never improved toward the older one, Emry. And he was more trouble than he was worth during our trek up from Salt Lake City, especially in the Shoshone camp. I think he ate his horse's grain rations from out of the saddle bag.

"Fact is, I've seen some things lately make me wonder if he isn't someway involved with the disappearin' gold shipments." Wilson paused in his comment and looked around the landscape, scanning carefully as though he expected they might be watched. Then he turned and faced Rob again.

"Anything ya could be more specific about?" Rob's interest in what the man had to say was rising.

"First off, there was a set of tracks I came across on the Salt Lake City route while headin' that way myself. Two riders followin' right after a freight wagon. The wagon tracks were heavy, but the riders' were light, probably fellas travelin' light to accompany the shipment, I figured. About two hours further along, here comes Emry an' Daniels, walking their mounts slowly back north. Emry said they'd been attacked while guardin' a shipment an' were now goin' into Bannack to report the robbery to the sheriff or whatever law they could find–maybe that judge fella.

"Said they'd been outnumbered, forced to throw down their guns. The two of them seemed fine, an' I had pressin' business in Salt Lake City, so I went on ahead. Couldn't help but notice how deep their horses tracked in the snow. Oh, an' he said they were walkin' the horses due to all the excitement of the robbery. Said they were afraid the animals might still spook pretty easily. This from a man who didn't care one iota for his mount just a few weeks earlier on the ride up from Salt Lake City. And that fella Daniels? He never said one word. Wouldn't look at me either.

"When I reached the scene of the robbery, the driver and his back-up were both dead, just like Emry said. But their guns were still in their hands, still loaded–neither of them had fired a shot. There were plenty of other tracks, probably from four or five more horsemen. The team pulling the wagon was gone. Those other horsemen and the team all rode away east. The tracks leading away were deep, too, about like the ones that Emry and Daniels made. Other than the two dead men, the wagon was empty. It was one of Conover's rigs. The gold crates were all busted open.

"It was warmer and the snow wasn't so deep as when I last passed that way. But the ground was frozen under the snow, so I figured the sheriff an' townsmen would take care of the bodies soon enough, once the Treasury men got to Bannack. I later found out that the robbery wasn't reported until two days afterwards.

"Emry never seems to be around when the action heats up, but he's always around right afterward. It turns out he knew that banker fella, Langford, before either of 'em arrived in the territories. Both have experience in banking and both are active members of the local Masons.

I got nothin' against the Masons–don't know much about 'em, havin' never been one myself, but I was taught to be mighty careful around bankers. Heard they weren't to be trusted since they're no better than money-changers. You know, like the ones in the Bible story? I'm tellin' ya, Rob, there's plenty about those Treasury men to make me nervous. Especially the one called Emry."

"I can see why y'd feel that way after hearin' yer tale. By the way, when was that robbery on the Salt Lake City trail?"

Wilson took his time to consider Rob's question. "Maybe about the end of February ... more than a week after we got back from Salt Lake City. It was before Plummer was elected sheriff, right in between when Hank Crawford left town and before folks organized an election."

Finn paused a long while before finally speaking. Wilson had given him a lot to think about. He said, "Thanks for telling me, John. It may be y've given me a key to some of what has been goin' on." He paused a second time, though not so long as the first, then continued, "If ya have the time, I could use yer help wi' another thing or two." Rob motioned for Wilson to follow him as he slowly resumed his uphill trek. Reaching into his vest pocket, he produced a small, clear red stone, one he had picked up while crossing this drainage last December. "Do ya ever see stones like this in the creeks around here, John?"

"Not everywhere I go, but they're pretty common in this district. Even more of 'em over in Alder Gulch. Don't get too excited, Rob. Not many are rubies. Mostly they're garnets. Some folks will take a few in trade, but they ain't worth much."

Rob took the stone as Wilson offered it back and returned it to the pocket from which it came. "What if the stones are of a different color, then?"

Wilson was more accustomed to the altitude and had taken the lead as they walked their way up the narrowing valley. At Rob's question, he turned himself part-way around and, with narrowed eyes, asked, "You mean clear, like glass? Have you found diamonds out here?"

"No. Ah don't think so. But Ah have found some green stones, an' some yellow ones. An Ah've seen others that are larger an' more deeply colored. Victor, the man that healed me from the bear attack, had a number of 'em."

"You mean the Salish chief?" Wilson's surprise was obvious in his voice.

"Ah guess he'd be the same one. Lives near Fort Owen. Ah need t' see him again, talk t' him about some things. Ah owe that man my life."

"You know, Rob, that's the town I call home these days. Victor an' I are friends. You're welcome to ride along with me when I head back."

Wilson had stopped when he reached the crest of the ridge they'd been climbing. By the time Rob caught up, he needed another breather. Looking into the valley below them, they could see the light glimmering from the small creek at its bottom. He could also see mounted riders riding away up that creek, following it to the Northeast. All but one of the dozen or so riders were Indians. The other rider was Timothy Emry, of that Rob was certain. Even at this distance he easily distinguished the Treasury Department's lead agent for the district.

With a quick hand motion to Wilson, the pair quietly moved away from the crest to avoid being spotted by those below. They looked around before creeping carefully back to a vantage point from which they could see, while not being seen. Rob was certain they'd not been spotted by the party below, and watched the group ride up the gulch and finally out of sight. He was surprised that Wilson had topped the ridge so carelessly, considering the man's years of experience.

"Those Indians were Sioux. I had plenty of dealin's with them when I was still with the Army. That fella with 'em looked a lot like Emry. Hard to tell at this distance. I can't be sure," Wilson admitted.

"Ah can be sure, John. And Ah am. That was Emry, all right. Ah can only guess at what he's doin', travelin' with a band of Indians."

"But what would Sioux be doin' all the way out here? Only ones we ever ran into were to the east, over in Dakota Territory, an' Minnesota." Wilson's face reflected the puzzlement in his questions.

"Ah don't know what they're here for, John. Ya heard about that business in Mankato day after Christmas?

When thirty-eight Sioux braves were hanged?  No matter what the government says, that'll keep the Sioux stirred up against white settlers for a long time.  Years, I'm guessin'.  Emry bein' with 'em really makes me wonder what's brewin'.  I think I'd better take ya up on yer offer to ride along to Fort Owen.  An' the sooner, the better.  But first, as long as we're already here, I want to take a look in that creek bottom.  I'm sure this is the same stream where I found these garnets last winter."

They climbed down the steep-sided valley, picking their footholds and handholds with care, yet still making a quick descent.  Again, because of experience, Wilson was more agile and reached the stream well ahead of Rob.  He had just finished taking a deep drink of the clear, sweet-tasting water when Rob stepped to the bank alongside the messenger.  Rob also slaked his thirst with handfuls of cold water, then reached back into the stream and brought forth two gleaming stones, both dark red in color and each as big around as a nailhead.

"That eyesight of yours really is somethin', ain't it?  I looked at that same spot an' never even noticed those."  Wilson shook his head slightly.  "I'll show you some real stones when we go back up into the Bitterroot, if there's time."

# CHAPTER THREE

# The Daze of War

*Saturday, July 18, 1863. Letterman Field Hospital, York Pike, Gettysburg, Pennsylvania.*

Union surgeon Dr. Henry James finished examining his patient followed by scribbling some notes onto a chart and commenting, "I'm amazed at your recovery, Corporal. Given the number of serious head injuries I've treated from men clubbing each other with rifle butts, there aren't many that surprise me any more. You're the exception. You'll have headaches and blurry vision for a time yet, maybe months. If you're as stout a fellow as you appear to be, and if your luck holds, those may pass entirely. And nothing, not even your jaw, is broken. You must have a thick skull. If you were to put in a few weeks here as a hospital orderly, you'd likely be paroled to the Western Territories after that. No promises, but a great likelihood. Are you willing to change dressings and bedpans for our Union wounded as well as your Confederate comrades?"

"I'd be happy to do all that an' more, sir, especially if it'd help my chances fer parole. I've no wish to spend time in a prison camp, that's fer sure." Corporal Patrick Murphy hoped he didn't seem over-eager at this opportunity. The facts were that he had been contemplating how best to escape this hospital and travel cross-country away from the war. He despised the ideas of being in a prisoner-of-war camp or returning to his regiment as a combatant. Parole would solve both of those worries for him.

"Well, I'll ask the Quartermaster and the head of the nursing staff to have a visit with you. They'll decide what work you'll be fit for and explain your oath, duties and what their expectations will be. You would be an honor-bound trustee. If your work was acceptable, I'm sure they would recommend your parole in short order. Good luck to you, son." The kindly doctor then hurried away to attend other patients and matters of administration. Like all those in his profession, he was tremendously over-worked during these first days following the three-day battle named after this city of Gettysburg. The miracle was that any of them had the energy and strength to continue with the heavy demands for their merciful services.

In the weeks which followed his interview with the head Sanitary Commission nurse and the Union Quartermaster Corps lieutenant, Patrick had multiple opportunities to doubt his decision to help their hospital efforts. Cleaning soiled, bed-ridden soldiers was distasteful, though he did get used to it. But he never got accustomed to assisting at amputations, during which he had to hold the screaming, squirming patients in place while their limbs were sawn off. There were insufficient anesthetic preparations available for them all. This was the duty he hated most. Each time he was notified that he had to perform this duty he thought of trying to escape. During the amputations, amid the blood and gore, the screaming and agony, his gorge rose in his throat each time. He always had to fight to keep his stomach from purging its contents.

There were rows and rows of large tents pitched in some kind of order that the military mind would appreciate. It was this conglomeration of temporary canvas shelters that came to be known as Camp Letterman, or Field Hospital Letterman, named after the US Army's head surgeon during, and immediately following the Gettysburg battle. Those rows of tents, with all manner of equipment, wagons, and sundry dunnage, tempted Murphy with thoughts of how easy it would be to hide among them. Then, after dark, a man might carefully make his way unnoticed by any of the few guards in place.

After a particularly bad day during which he assisted at eight or nine amputations–he lost count–during which two men died, and then having to help dispose of severed limbs and corpses, he nearly bolted. He did not understand how anyone could volunteer for this duty. It certainly was not for him. As he was returning from dumping the last of the cut-off limbs, Patrick looked up and down the streets between the tents considering his best route of escape. He was confident he could make it out of the camp and beyond.

But in the end, he kept his word, did his duties as assigned. With all the misery and suffering he witnessed in his orderly duties, Patrick Murphy was increasingly aware of just how fortunate he had been to have survived his role in Picket's Charge.

Among Patrick's easier chores were those of changing bed linens and assisting the wounded to eat. While changing linens he could allow his mind to wander some, and his favorite daydreams were imagining himself back home in Ireland or reunited with his older sister Bridget. Watching the badly wounded men while he helped them with their food evoked deep feelings of sympathy for them and at the same time a growing anger that so many had been called upon to give up so much in this war.

Murphy was not yet well enough to carry the litters on which the most severe cases were moved to trains, which would take them to hospitals or camps in the other Northern states. He still had bouts of dizziness occurring at random times. His ear, neck and shoulder on his right side, near where the gunstock had struck, still bothered him painfully. Perhaps of greater concern were his blackouts–times when he would lose touch with the happenings around him. These never lasted for more than a few moments, and seemed to be occurring less frequently.

Patients being transported were the most serious cases and the risk of being jolted or dropped could not be allowed.

Patrick did not have exact information as to when he might be paroled, but hoped it would be soon. Rumors had spread among the Confederate patients and orderlies that the number of paroles was being cut back. This increased his concern that he wouldn't be paroled; that instead he might be sent to a prison camp. Worry kept him from sleeping some nights. He hoped he had not misplaced his trust in these Union medical people, and clung to his hopes for a better tomorrow.

* * *

*Wednesday, July 22, 1863. Mabie Brothers Circus camp along the northwestern shore of Lake Delavan, Wisconsin. Late afternoon, the circus workers seated for their evening meal in the big tent.*

"Alright, everybody, listen up. Right after dinner tonight we're packing up into the wagons and pulling out. We need to be west of town before the sun sets. Then we'll go on for a while in the dark, just to get a good start to the trip." Jeremiah Mabie's clear voice addressed the large body assembled at dinner.

A voice rang out, "Where we headed, boss?"

"We'll be in Madison for a week, then to Platteville for a week, followed by Prairie-du-chien and LaCrosse.

We'll cross the Mississippi there on our way to Minneapolis. We'll be in Minneapolis for at least four weeks, longer if the crowds hold, and decide our next stops from what happens there. If all goes as well as we hope, we'll loop down through Iowa, and back up through central and northern Illinois. Expect to be back here before the snow flies. Should all make ourselves pretty good money with this trip."

Though it was inaudible in all but a few instances, a general sigh of relief passed through the seated throng. Trouble with the Sioux since the hangings in Mankato had been less than people expected. Working in Minnesota and Iowa seemed safe enough. No one wanted to pass into Missouri due to the ongoing tensions there.

John Finn was seated next to the elephant handler who was also his boss in the circus. Stewart Craven was a good man, and the only man living who could safely handle the circus's killer elephant, Romeo. The huge beast had already killed three people in separate episodes of outrage. Juliet, by comparison, was not only much smaller than her male counterpart, she was much more tractable. Craven was teaching young John the basics of elephant handling with Juliet. John was sure he could and should be handling Romeo.

Circus people had enormous appetites due to the amount of physically demanding labor they were expected to perform on a daily basis. The Mabie brothers believed that one of the important elements contributing to the success of their operation was that they fed their hired help exceptionally well. After nearly forty minutes devoted to eating everything put before them, the last of the troupe were done.

Using the clanger of the dinner bell to be heard above the noise, Jerry Mabie again called out, "All right. Everybody lend a hand. Let's get this show on the road!"

*  *  *

*Monday, July 27th, 1863. Two miles south of the Fort Owen settlement in the Bitterroot valley.*

Their ride north had been entirely pleasant. Since the wagon they borrowed from Crisman had a padded cushion on the bench seat, Rob and Lonnie were rather enjoying the scenery from their seated positions. The wagon had a load that was easy enough for Bricks to pull, while having enough weight to keep it from hopping around much as it traveled up the rough track into the Bitterroot Valley. As their pace was slow enough to be leisurely, this was more of a gentle exercise than a workout for the big horse. Roxie was happy enough to follow along behind the wagon on her tether with an empty saddle on her back—ready in case the need arose. Neither Rob nor Lonnie would ever forget their first experience in the western mountains. Roxie had been attacked by and rescued from a mountain lion. Also during that eventful trip, a young woman in their company had been killed and Rob seriously injured by a grizzly bear before Lonnie had been able to kill the bear.

John Wilson rode alongside the wagon, being his usual, companionable self and obviously quite comfortable in the surroundings leading to his home. The threesome passed their travel-time together sharing stories, jokes and anecdotes as they felt the urge to do so. In all they were having a fine time together.

They had spent their first night out from Bannack at the place Wilson promised to show them, a place where they could find large, pink quartz crystals just by digging in the soft earth. They had tethered the horse team and wagon and walked up the remaining elevation to their destination. The view from high on the mountain was spectacular, even compared to the many other spectacular views Rob and Lonnie had seen during their travels in the West. They were further rewarded when they found several crystals without great effort. Marveling at these natural wonders put them all in the best possible spirits. There were no distractions of greed or temptation in this beautiful mountain setting. It was quite a bit colder than in the valley below, a refreshing break from the summer's heat.

Before the sun set that first night their camp was made, the horses cared for, dinner was eaten and the dishes cleaned and put away. The men wrapped their crystal finds in scraps of cloth and placed them carefully into the wagon bed, along with the goods already packed that they were transporting to Fort Owen. Some of the items in their load had been ordered from George Crisman by customers living in the Fort Owen area, and these three were merely performing a neighborly delivery service in exchange for the use of the wagon. Some supplies were for their personal use. Still other items were brought along to give to their Salish Indian friends as gifts, including several crates of canned food. Rob thought that the Imperial Brand of tinned oysters he brought along would surprise and delight Victor. This brand from the Thomas Kensett & Company of Baltimore was Rob's favorite, and he sincerely hoped others might enjoy them as well. Rob was really looking forward to again seeing the Salish medicine man who had saved his life. He also planned to give his share of the crystals and the clear stones he had found to the healer, thinking that the crystals might have some use to Victor in his healing arts. In addition to being a medicine man, Victor was also a chief among his people.

Not forgetting Sarah Ogden, who also helped with Rob's treatment last fall, he had brought along a book and a small hand mirror for her. He also remembered his other traveling companions from that time, the Salish brother and sister duo, Oce-asay and Tanehee. For Oce-asay he brought along a well-crafted Bowie knife in a leather sheath, thinking that it would be useful to the young hunter/warrior. For Tanehee he had selected a bolt of colorful cloth for her to use according to her wishes.

Traveling continuously during most of the long daylight hours brought them close to their destination two days after leaving the crystal campsite. The uneventful trek took them through the majestic scenery in this part of the Territories. Rob repeatedly thought to himself that he could be entirely happy and at peace in a place such as this. Lonnie had similar thoughts and remarked repeatedly about the natural beauty surrounding them as they traveled along. The rugged Bitterroot range of mountains was on their left rising impressively and covered with immense fir and pine forests. The Bitterroot River coursed happily along on their right and the Sapphire Range was further right marking the eastern slope of the valley.

They all kept alert for anything that might come at them from the forested mountainsides or from the treed and brushy banks of the river and its tributary creeks. Each man regularly ran hands over his favored gun–just checking to make sure they were still at the ready. Lonnie held his coach-styled shotgun across his knees while Rob drove. Rob now carried a Colt US Army revolver in a hip holster and had his Sharps rifle in the wagon bed. Wilson's preferred armament was a late model Spencer repeating rifle.

Wilson removed his hat and waved it back and forth over his head as they approached the little fort, yelling "Hello to the fort" repeatedly, so as not to surprise anyone who had not seen them approaching.

* * *

*Tuesday, July 28th, 1863. A narrow canyon south of the main East–West trail between Bannack and Alder Gulch.*

The band of twelve Sioux Indian braves halting for the day in a sheltered area west and south of the new diggings in Alder Gulch was unusual for at least two reasons. The first being that Sioux Indians were seldom found this far west and the second being that their leader, or guide, was none other than Timothy Emry, Treasury Agent. Emry was dressed in his usual dapper style: a suit of clothes with a matching bowler hat and gentleman's boots–his outfit immaculate, as always. He had black hair and a well-groomed mustache; always spoke with a clear, confident voice. He had noticed about himself that he had an uncanny likeness to Henry Plummer. When Nathan Langford observed that fact aloud after a Masonic Lodge meeting one evening, several other men chimed in their agreement. It was remarked that, excepting for Emry's smaller stature, they could be brothers, even twins. Other than the obvious difference in size, Emry's own comment that "I don't usually carry a pistol, don't like them", was the only other distinguishing difference mentioned.

There was no coincidence in Emry's being with a band of Sioux Indian braves this far into the Western Territories, however. Emry had taken considerable precautions to locate and hire these particular members of the Sioux nation, so there was no mystery to him regarding their presence here. Shortly following the Mankato Massacre, he had used his former banking position and personal contacts in the southern Minnesota region to locate Sioux braves who were seeking to avenge what had been done to their tribes. They needed to be hot-blooded enough to want revenge, yet level-headed enough to take direction from a white man willing to pay them while helping them to achieve that goal. Not many young braves possessed these traits together. Emry felt fortunate to have these dozen Sioux in his employ, and the two among them who understood English became his de facto sergeants for the renegade band.

The Indians, for their part, had no reason not to trust this man. His trade goods were of high quality and he never shorted them on a deal. They knew him by name as Henry Plummer; he made sure all twelve of them were capable of saying one or both of the names he used. His two subordinate leaders among the Sioux always called him Plummer.

The Sioux braves were also pleased with this man whom they knew as Plummer because, in addition to showing them where they could kill white men who were greedily taking over their lands for the yellow metal, he allowed them to scalp or maim the corpses if they pleased. They had made more raids than they could have hoped; they were tiring of this way of living. Several of the older braves were already thinking of returning to their lands in

Minnesota, though they were not planning to return to the reservation there.

"Plummer" showed them good, well-hidden campsites and provided them with plenty of food, even though it was not to their particular liking. They found the cans containing it to be troublesome. Hunting was good in these valleys and mountains. "Plummer" was not their chief, but since he was providing these opportunities to avenge their massacred brothers, they took orders from him. Among Emry's orders to his hired band of robbers was that they avoid white settlements. They were to remain out of sight other than when ordered to attack a shipment.

Though they were armed with rifles and shotguns, the Sioux only used the firearms during attacks on the whites' shipments. These braves hunted venison using bows and they were surprisingly accurate at putting arrows into the vital organs of their intended game. So much so, Emry wondered if he shouldn't have them use the primitive weapons in their attacks. Best to not take chances, he thought. It had not been easy finding these twelve; it would be harder to replace them. The guns were much more efficient and gave his Indian "road-agents" an even-or-better chance of surviving the encounters that he arranged. And he loved the idea that the name of Henry Plummer was being used as their leader. He hated the man for being slightly better-looking and taller than himself. Those were among his reasons for keeping Plummer out of the Masons.

Emry had no similar feeling of satisfaction when he recalled his partner James Daniels. Daniels had been a good enough young fellow, wanting to please his superiors in the Treasury Department, including Emry. Emry figured he would mold the young man to do his bidding, and nearly succeeded. Or so he thought.

Then, after Emry and he had assisted in a gold shipment robbery, Daniels informed him he could no longer keep quiet about Emry's activities, even though he, too, had been involved in them. Daniels told Emry this on their way back to Bannack. Less than two hours after Daniels' pronouncement, the Sioux had killed and scalped the man–at Plummer's (Emry's) order, of course. Daniels' remains were hidden by the Indians. Emry neither knew nor cared where.

Timothy Emry was pleased with how his plans and operations were turning out, and could not let a small detail such as the life of one underling sidetrack his enterprises. He was accumulating a good deal of gold for himself, with even more potential in the future, and no one suspected him of any wrong-doing. Of this last fact he was certain, now that Daniels had been silenced. It was just too bad for Daniels that his upbringing and conscience got in the way of following Emry's better way of life.

Emry had already sent a telegram to Washington notifying them that Daniels had gone missing and that he would prefer to find and hire a replacement locally. He was still awaiting a response from his superiors in the East.

* * *

*Thursday, July 30, 1863. The Salish Village near Fort Owen, in the northern Bitteroot Valley of Idaho Territory. Evening on the night of the full moon.*

Victor, Sarah, Oce-asay and Tanehee each made Rob feel welcome in their village when they saw him again. Rob was overjoyed at their small reunion—he felt intensely attached to these four people. Victor had been directly responsible for the use of his healing knowledge that saved Rob's life. Each of the others had helped the medicine man, and Rob, with their own contributions to his survival and recovery. Oce-asay and Tanehee were grateful toward the big Irishman who had fought so selflessly against a grizzly bear to save their sister's life. They recognized and honored such courage in another, despite the fact that his efforts had been in vain. They would never forget him.

The young adult Salish brother and sister were similarly happy to see Lonnie again. It was Lonnie's close-range shotgun blast that ended the fight with the bear, thus sparing further deaths or injuries, and whose knowledge of healing aided Victor's work. His action against the attacking mother bear last fall had shown his good heart and brave spirit.

These six were seated around a ring of rocks containing their small campfire. This year's drought had not been so deep as many, but the Salish were careful people, taking no chances of starting the forests ablaze. Several other local residents were present, including John Wilson, and Michel Ogden, Sarah's father.

Also present at the campfire was the Jesuit priest, Father Anthony Ravalli. Victor had invited the priest, who gladly accepted the invitation, largely because of their close religious attachment. Victor had embraced many of the Catholic teachings and been baptized; Ravalli and he shared healing practices and remedies to the benefit of all people living within a growing radius of the fort and St. Mary's Mission church. Their successes with healing arts were well-known.

Victor was a chief among the Bitterroot Salish people. He had, in fact, been one of the signatories of the Hellgate Treaty enacted eight years earlier, creating the first Flathead Indian Reservation. He later learned that he and the other chiefs had been tricked by clever language changes and deceitful translations of the treaty's clauses. Since he was not one to cling to old wrongs, Victor did not fuss much about the shabby treatment he and his people received at that time. But he did not forget the treachery it revealed and learned that not all whites could be trusted, especially those with government positions. Victor was a wise man.

As darkness deepened, the sun having set more than a half hour earlier, those circling the fire instinctively moved in closer for both the light and the heat the flames provided. Even in summer, these valleys cooled swiftly once the sun was behind the western mountain ranges. The moonlight was sufficient to see clearly, yet the attraction of the flames was ancient. People stared into the flickering tongues of bright yellow-orange in a nearly hypnotic state and continued their slow, deliberate talking that accompanied such moments.

Michel Ogden did not utter a single word that night. Others noticed that he seldom blinked and had been thus entranced even before the fire was full and the darkness complete. His daughter Sarah was his primary caregiver, so she had seen this behavior regularly ever since her father's head injury two years earlier.

Acting upon a discreet signal from Victor, Sarah began prodding her father to stir himself and stand up. When he did so, she herded him off in the direction of their teepee. As soon as they were satisfied at the progress Michel Ogden was making toward his night's lodging, John Wilson and Victor rose from their places and invited Rob and Lonnie to accompany them to Victor's home. Father Ravalli joined them on the short walk to the teepee and was ushered into its opening by Victor, after he had graciously signaled Rob, Lonnie, and John to enter before himself. These five men then seated themselves around a much smaller fire ring in the center of the enclosure. This had burned down to embers and cast just enough light for them to see.

A few moments later, the group was again joined by

Sarah Ogden, who settled herself between Victor and the priest with all the confidence of any adult participant at a meeting. The priest crossed himself in the Catholic tradition and said a prayer in Latin. He then nodded to Victor, who bowed his head and spoke in a tongue unknown to Finn or Walters–he was praying in the Salish language. When he finished, Victor raised his head and looked around the circle, his eyes briefly searching the eyes of each participant. Finally, he focused on Rob's face before speaking in English.

"We have many important things for talking here this night. My heart is full this night, but not heavy. I am happy to see my brother Man-who-Kills-Himself-with-Bear standing strong. Rob Finn honors us with his visit."

Rob had no idea where this was going, so was caught off guard. His natural humility came forward as did a broad and happy smile that covered his big face. His Irish emotions threatened to overwhelm him; he felt the lump form in his throat and knew he would not be able to speak without his voice breaking. As taught by his father from childhood, he chose silence for the moment, but nodded his appreciation toward his host.

Father Ravalli also nodded in agreement, but it was Sarah Ogden who spoke next. Her voice, though full of emotion, was even and calm. She said, "Rob-Finn, Lonnee: you have seen my father, how he looks but does not see. He is not the same man as before his accident with the horse. He remembers only some things. He cannot do numbers any longer. He is peaceful and sleeps long hours. He is still a good man." Sarah hesitated and took a deep breath before continuing on.

"What I tell now is known to few. It is a matter of great concern for us. A matter needing great trust. Because of your actions with the bear and now returning to us with gifts, we know we can trust you. John Wilson: we have learned to trust you in our years together." At this point both Victor and the priest nodded their approval, while looking around at the three men Sarah had just named.

"My father got the gold fever from his trader work for the Hudson's Bay Company. Then he found some gold when we still lived at Fort Connah. He spent much time looking for it, then hiding what he found. My mother and brothers and sisters all worried that he would go crazy. We had seen it in others before, among the white men that came through looking for gold. My father told us to tell no one of his great secret–so we did not. He found and hid gold for many, many months.

"My mother and I saw him hiding his gold when we were gathering plants one day. He did not see us. We were afraid to tell him–afraid he might have gold fever anger toward us. We never told anyone where we saw him. Then, after he was hurt and could not remember much, we went and looked at his hiding place. It held much gold. We were afraid it would bring trouble, even more than it had already. It has been a long time now, and

Father does not remember. I think he never will. I think that is best.

"I do not think this gold is a good thing for our people. I did not think it is good to leave it where Father hid it. I was afraid men would learn of it and come after it. Mother and I moved the gold to a better place away from the trading post. Mother agreed with me and we talked to Victor and Father Ravalli about this. My brothers and sisters know nothing of this. We want this gold gone away. We want you to take it. It can be yours! Please take it away from us. Take it to where it will not harm our people."

This announcement stunned Finn, Walters, and even Wilson. None of them had any inkling about the hidden trove of gold; none of them imagined being trusted with a large treasure or the responsibility attached to it. Everyone in the teepee was quiet, waiting.

It was Victor who next broke the silence. "We have talked much since you arrived three days ago. We (he motioned with his right hand to indicate Sarah, the priest, himself) think this is best for our people. You will help?"

Rob was seated between Lonnie and John. He clearly saw the looks of concern on their faces, and knew his own face was betraying his concerns. The main worry in his mind was what to do with a quantity of gold once it was away from these mountain valleys. Should they turn it into the Treasury Department? Tell Pinkerton? Hide it away for themselves? Each possibility raised its own set of problems.

Father Ravalli spoke up before any of the trio had the chance to gather their thoughts. "Your hesitation confirms what we already knew about the three of you. You have concerns about your own souls, about your own integrity. You see the great responsibility of this request. You are not greedy men looking only for your own well-being. You are the right men to handle this problem for these people."

"We'll need t' talk this over some, Father," Rob sighed. "'Tis not a matter t' be taken lightly, that much is for sure."

Finn's comment was followed by heads nodding agreement and a few whispers. The meeting broke up and everyone went outside again. Even though it was August, they felt the crisp cool air–smelled its freshness. The moon was well up in the sky, and the complete lack of clouds allowed the stars to stand out against deep blue heavens above them. Rob thought, "I've never seen a clearer, more beautiful night sky, anywhere." He might have been surprised to know that Walters and Wilson also had exactly that thought in their minds. Aloud , he announced, "Let's go have a talk about things."

Walters and Wilson nodded in the affirmative as the three strode across the small village to the teepee in which Finn and Walters were staying. The village campfire had been extinguished and no one else was about.

It took Wilson only a few moments to stoke the fire in the teepee to the point where it gave off an agreeable amount of both light and heat. He hunkered down at the fire's edge facing the opening to the lodge. "Rob, I hope you won't mind my saying so, but there's no way we can let that scoundrel Emry know about this!" The words came out a bit more emphatically than Wilson had intended, such was the strength of his feeling about the matter.

"Yer opinion is important t' this decision, John, and I happen t' agree wi' ya. I'm further thinkin' that this best be kept from the rest of the Treasury Department an' even the agency for now. The first thing t'do is decide if we even want t' get involved. This could become trouble for us all." Rob's troubled facial expression matched his tone.

Lonnie added, "Of course we could walk away, but I don't think any of us could live with ourselves if we did that. They're countin' on us to deliver them from this precious trouble." Wilson and Finn nodded their agreement with Walters' statement. They each saw this as a duty owed, and none of the three would shirk it.

"I'm in for the whole hitch–these people are my friends," Wilson said. "But then what do we do with the gold? Where do we take it? We don't even know how much we're talkin' about yet, do we?"

Rob looked at each of his two friends then added, "Someplace no one would ever expect us t' take it. And soon. It's too easy for word t' get out about a matter like this. We need t' start tomorrow, or the next day at the latest. I have an idea where we might take it, but I'm not sure you two will like it."

# CHAPTER FOUR

# Gracious Victors

*Friday, July 31, 1863. Fort Owen, Idaho Territory, shortly after breakfast.*

Say what you might about Allan Pinkerton, the man was loyal to his friends. It was George McClellan, the "young Napoleon" general of the US Army, who had arranged Pinkerton's position as head of spying and intelligence gathering in 1861. When President Lincoln relieved McClellan from his post late in 1862, Pinkerton resigned his appointed post within the administration as a show of allegiance. It was a political display, since the Pinkerton agency and operatives continued to supply detective and spying services to the North on a contract basis. If anything, revenues to the agency increased for a time, later drawing the attention, investigation, and disapproval of several members of the U.S. Congress.

Major General Joseph Hooker took control of the US Army following McClellan's removal and, among other things, Hooker ordered the establishment of a new military department, the Bureau of Military Information. Under the capable leadership of a former Pinkerton agent, John Babcock, this group also provided spying services for the

Lincoln government. Babcock, together with two other of the Bureau's operatives were presently watching things in the gold fields of the West. They had lately left the mining town of Bannack to further observe another group leaving that town. The three BMI operatives took care not to be spotted while following the group ahead of them.

The BMI men were following their orders from Hooker, which were similar to those of the Pinkertons: to keep watch on all gold shipments or any unusual or suspicious activity in the mining districts. The wagon leaving Bannack traveling north seemed suspicious enough to them. Their latest telegraphed orders from Washington, D.C. added that they should also keep careful track of all movements by Treasury Department operative Timothy Emry, to learn what they could about his missing partner, James Daniels.

After following discreetly for five days, they had nearly decided that this small party was no longer worth watching. Then, while cleaning up their small camp high on a mountain shoulder overlooking Fort Owen, Babcock and his men spotted the three travelers with their wagon leaving the settlement, again heading north. Four Indians on horseback were leading the way. The BMI operatives finished breaking camp and mounted their horses, again trailing the Pinkertons and company from a distance.

\* \* \*

Rob's two companions were pleased with the decision the three of them had reached–to take on the burden and responsibility of the gold trove, or simply "the trove", as they referred to it among themselves now. Many doubts still haunted them. None had admitted to the others his own private concern regarding his personal thoughts of temptation. Gold really could have a strong influence on the way a man viewed his surroundings and his pards. Yet each of these three knew himself well enough to know that the Salish leader, Victor, had trusted them for their behavior toward Indians. And each man was as certain as any man can be of another that his two fellows would not cause problems. Though each did his own thinking about himself and the other two, all three concluded that this undertaking would be successful.

In addition to considering options of where to take or hide the trove, they also had to figure out how to get the gold to whatever destination they chose. It was a blessing they had Crisman's wagon along. Though it was not the heavy-duty freight wagon they would have preferred for such a job, it was much better than having to do without a wheeled conveyance. They could reinforce the box and axles should the load require it. It seemed best to all that they leave at once to survey their cargo. Sarah, Victor and the priest wanted them to plan the actual recovery of the gold to take place during darkness.

Allowing two-and-a-half days travel to reach Fort Connah meant they would arrive the third afternoon after the full moon. They would need to time their loading by the sunset and moonrise and to work quickly. Victor and Sarah were consulted to see if others could help with the task, persons whom they trusted from their own little circle. Victor and Sarah would go along and help, of course, but in Victor's estimation there would need to be two more strong young workers along to assist.

Victor and Sarah decided upon Oce-asay and Tanehee, the brother and sister guides who had accompanied Rob and Lonnie the preceding fall. None would disagree with these two for the job. They were well-known by all, including John Wilson, and were trusted, hard-working young adults. The two of them readily agreed to the plan–they were eager to help once they learned of the matter.

Having off-loaded all the goods they'd brought for delivery, the wagon bed was empty, save for their essential personal gear. The Salish rode their horses, as would Wilson. Bricks again provided the draft power and Roxie followed behind the wagon except for those occasions that Lonnie felt like riding. On the second morning out from Fort Owen, they decided to try pairing Bricks and Roxie together pulling the wagon and using a makeshift "tree" attached to the forward underside of the wagon as a yoke. The rig had been designed and hastily constructed by John Wilson before they left the fort. He had seen and assembled similar arrangements during his time with the US Army.

Despite the height and size differences, the two horses teamed surprisingly well together after a few wedges were placed and the tack was adjusted. This measure was being taken in case the laden wagon was heavy enough to require two horses to pull it. Their hope was that the load would not require both animals to haul it. By the time this party reached the crossing at Post Creek just outside Fort Connah, the wagon was moving along smoothly to the routine and rhythm that Roxie and Bricks had established.

Rob was again touched by the intelligent and gentle nature of the beautiful black gelding. Rob was aware that, though Roxie was a fine horse, Bricks had made nearly all the adjustments to gait and timing in order to make the pairing work. That was not something that can be taught. Bricks did it because he wanted to, and he made it happen himself. What a magnificent beast was this horse!

Since neither Rob nor Lonnie had been to this trading post before, it made sense to show the layout of things to them before their evening meal and before darkness fell, when the real work would begin. Sarah and Victor took turns explaining the history of the small post, and that it was the last of the Hudson's Bay Company locations in the region. The Company no longer operated it, but it was yet seen by many as an outpost of the English empire here.

Sarah pointed out the sleeping room she shared with her brothers and sisters when they all lived here. Rob and

Lonnie could see that they must have been tucked in "like sardines". Probably kept them warmer in winter; perhaps they slept outdoors in summer.

Time for their supper came and all happily and gratefully ate together the meal that Wilson, Oce-asay and Tanehee had prepared. This company was in fine spirits: enjoying the food, the companionship, the fine weather. They cleaned up after themselves and then waited for the sun to fully drop behind the western mountains before following Sarah to locate her father's gold stash.

None of them were certain how much time they would have for working before the moonlight would be bright enough to expose their efforts, so they all moved quickly to complete hitching the team and preparing tools and the wagon. Sarah knew right where she was going, despite the dark, and, after crossing the creek at a narrow place between two stands of cottonwood trees, Sarah led them nearly due east toward the base of the mountains. Her hand finally rose up, signaling everyone to halt, which they did. Sarah communicated what she needed in whispers, the result being that Rob, Lonnie, John and Oce-asay were again following her with shovels while Victor and Tanehee kept watch for any who might be approaching.

The cairn chamber that the men dug open at Sarah's direction was long and low, perhaps eight feet long by a foot high. It was covered with turves of sod, probably done years earlier, and difficult to see in broad daylight. A perfect hiding spot, it blended well with the run of the land around it. If anyone did notice it, it was about the right size for an ancient funeral mound–sacred among those cultures that used them and respected by those that didn't.

The work party dug three openings into the low, north-south running mound: one on each end and one in the middle on the west side. It was immediately apparent to Sarah that the contents had not been disturbed. The cache contained four sturdy wooden crates which had not rotted, and ten metal strongboxes. Lying on their bellies outside the three openings and reaching inside until they could feel one another's hands, the men thus also emptied the trove of a number of large canvas bags. These were somewhat worse for the wear of being buried, though the many hide-bound leather pokes they contained were in fine condition.

By now the moon was rising, advancing rapidly as the mountaintops southeast of their position became alight in its ascension. Aware that little time remained before they would be bathed in moonlight, the workers continued their fast pace. They were still in the mountain shadows as they finished removing the last of the hoard onto the wagon and replacing the rocks and turves on the hiding place.

When their work was finished, the waning moon was high enough and bright enough to engulf the worksite in its white light. Though the ground was disturbed from their efforts, a casual passerby would not have given it a second look even in daylight.

Victor, Rob, and Sarah were satisfied that the chamber had been emptied and the hiding place restored to its former natural-looking condition. That all the gold had been successfully removed was also a certainty. What most of them did not know was that their activities that night had been observed. The others would have been unnerved if, like Rob, they were aware of three pairs of human eyes watching from less than a quarter-mile away.

Clouds were moving in from the west. Eventually they would block the moon's light and make the trek back to the fort a little more challenging. The darkness would hide the work party and their watchers from each other.

As the wagon carrying the gold headed back toward the creek crossing, a light drizzle fell. It made just enough noise as it fell on the cottonwood leaves to cover the sound of their passage.

Reaching the small cluster of buildings that made up Fort Connah took no time at all. It had stopped raining which made the chore of guarding the wagon less onerous for those tasked with taking turns at that duty. Rob took the first watch. He wanted to give his senses, especially his eyes, the opportunity to better ascertain who was following them. The sky was again becoming cloudless as the small storm continued to the east. Rob figured that the returning brightness would give him the visual advantage over their adversaries. Then, after a couple more hours, the moon would be down.

\* \* \*

*Friday, August 7, 1863. Breakfast in Letterman Field Hospital, Gettysburg, Pennsylvania.*

A better tomorrow for Patrick Murphy finally arrived. He was seated at the bedside of a young Yank private, Billy Adams, whose right arm at been removed at the shoulder. Adams' damaged left hand and forearm were tightly wrapped in the medical hope that they might mend well enough to one day again be of use to the nineteen-year-old amputee. The young patient was in fine spirits this morning, especially for one who had lost so much. Billy was propped up on his cot, enjoying the company of the orderly feeding him oatmeal. Though they wore the uniforms of enemies, they'd become friendly during Billy's recuperation. This was partly due to their closeness in age–Patrick was only three years Billy's senior–and partly due to the fact that young Adams was from Wisconsin, the state in which Patrick's sister lived.

Patrick had asked many questions about Billy's home state and always listened patiently to the young soldier's answers. From his glowing descriptions of the surrounding farms, neighbors and towns, Billy's love for his hometown of Walworth was genuine. That Billy knew of and had been to the nearby town of Darien thrilled Patrick beyond measure. Darien was the town where his sister, Bridget, and her husband farmed.

Both patient and orderly were startled by the lieutenant's voice. "Murphy, I'll see you outside the mess tent as soon as you finish with your patient. It's time to discuss your parole."

A mumbled "Yes, sir" was all Murphy could manage as he tried to stand and come to attention.

"At ease, soldier, no need for formality now," from the lieutenant settled Murphy back down to resume feeding his friend.

In addition to surprise, Billy looked worried when he asked, "So this will mean good-bye? You'll be sent out West, away from the war, eh? I sure wish I was going with you, Patrick." The look in Billy's eyes told his sincere longing beyond what his words said.

"They'll be sending you home in no time, Billy. Soon as yer hand an' arm are healed a little more, y'll be going back to Wisconsin. Wait an' see. It'll happen just that way." Patrick carefully used a napkin to dab away the gruel that had slid onto Billy's chin.

"I'd rather be headed out West with you, Patrick. My folks in Walworth won't have much use for a one-armed cripple who can't do a day's worth of farm work." Billy's head drooped; his former high spirits gone in the instant he realized the truth of his own words. "I could be some use to you in the mining districts. I know I could help!" His rising voice showed his desperation not to be left behind.

Many parolees went into the Western Territories to try trapping or mining as a way to keep their oaths to "remain West of the warring States." Their motivation to fulfill the oath was excellent–death was the penalty for violating it.

"We don't know what's going to happen with either of us yet, Billy. Take it easy. All the lieutenant said was that it was time to talk about my parole. Don't worry about it. I'll tell ya everything I hear when I bring yer dinner." Patrick was all calm outwardly, but inside he was excited at the prospect of getting away from the war. Still, he felt genuine compassion for Adams and his plight. And he knew it was no use to argue. Billy had a valid point: he might not be much use on his family's farm and might be uncomfortable with those who had known him when he was whole. "Anyway, don't worry so, Billy. Things have a way of workin' out is what my Da always said."

"Easy for you to say, with two good arms an' legs." Billy's sullenness was understandable under the circumstances, so Patrick ignored the comment.

"I'll see you in a couple of hours, Billy." Patrick gathered up the plate, bowl, and utensils into the napkin Billy had used and then strode toward the tent opening nearest the mess tent. A wave of excitement washed over him as he imagined himself being free to travel away from the accursed war.

He found the lieutenant easily enough. As Murphy passed through the walkway separating the mess tent from those nearest it, the tall officer made eye contact and nodded toward him. Murphy deposited the dirty dishes and napkin in the designated receptacles before catching up with the officer. They walked easily along together, Murphy following just behind until they reached the partitioned-off areas used as offices. Lieutenant Webber seated himself behind the tiny field desk, and motioned for Patrick to take a seat opposite him.

The lieutenant got right into it. "You've done commendable work for us here, Corporal, and we appreciate it. We could certainly use you around here for a while longer. But that might not be fair to you. The Federal government of the United States is planning to cut out paroles such as yours altogether. It's a tough choice for us to let you go–we're so short of help in the hospital–but, as I said, it's the only fair thing to do. Your papers are here, already signed and ready to go. In addition to the parole document, there's a rail voucher that'll get you to St. Louis. After that you must get yourself west of Missouri as quickly as possible. Don't stop to visit anywhere. If found to be in violation of any of these instructions, you can be arrested, tried and executed. Do you have any questions, Murphy? Now's the time to ask 'em if you do."

"I'm happy enough to leave, sir, and appreciate all you've done for me. There's one other thing I could do that might help you out if you'd allow it." Murphy's voice cracked but once from his nervousness. "I could take Private Adams with me, and look after him. With his arm gone, he won't be returned to duty, will he?"

The shock of what Murphy was suggesting registered on Webber's face. He asked, "If I'm understanding you correctly, Corporal, you're volunteering to act as personal orderly for a severely wounded Union soldier? One who is unable to defend himself?"

"I mean him no harm, sir. We've become friends, er, after a fashion. I think he'd be happy to come with me." Patrick's anxiety rose again, and he was sweating heavily under his tunic.

"I'll tell you what, Murphy. If young Adams wants to go with you, that will be arranged. And you're right. You would be helping us out, at the same time you'd be helping your friend." He wrote a few lines on a blank form, signed it, then rose and signaled Murphy to follow. When they reached the point at which they could enter the tent containing Private Adams' cot, the lieutenant instructed Murphy to wait for him until he returned.

He was back a few minutes later with another orderly, this one in Union blue, and the lieutenant had a smile on his face. When he was close enough to Murphy to be heard in low voice, he said, "We'll need to take care in talking to Adams. Other patients nearby might get agitated if they learn what's planned. It'll do none of them any favor to get excited about something that doesn't concern them directly and that won't be happening for them. So I want you to help me keep Adams quiet while we all attend to this business. And the sooner we get it done, and the two of you on your way, the better."

Patrick could easily imagine the deep disappointment other wounded soldiers might feel when one among them was getting an early chance to return home. He nodded his agreement to the lieutenant as the three of them ducked into the tent on their mission of cautious but joyful mercy. They managed to inform Adams of the plan, gathering him and his things with a minimum of noise or excitement. The lieutenant led the foursome out a different opening of the tent, then along several grassy pathways.

When they reached the York Pike, they were greeted by a small, simple wagon, with a Union soldier driving one horse between the shafts. The bed of the wagon, (which was really more of a cart), was covered with burlap sacking and a couple of blankets for padding. After helping Billy up into the back, Patrick turned to the lieutenant, who explained while the other orderly helped Murphy out of his Confederate tunic. "This is the tunic you must wear in keeping with your parole oath. Murphy, if you are found without it anywhere before you reach the Territories you can be executed. Do you understand that?" He placed strong emphasis on the word 'must' as well as the four words of his query.

The coat that replaced Murphy's uniform tunic was of simple canvas and had the word "Parolee" painted in bold letters between the shoulders on the back. "Indeed I do, sir. I won't be forgettin' it, either." He was shaking with the emotion of the moment.

"Alright then, men. I can't allow you any guns to take along, and you're not to be found with any while you are still in the States. There's some provisions and water for you in the back of the wagon. We must finish up this business here quickly, so that's it. Good-bye and good luck to the both of you." He offered Murphy his hand in parting and started to do the same for Adams and then realized his mistake–the youngster's hand and arm were still bound against his body to immobilize them. He thought to ask if Murphy knew how much longer Adams needed to be kept swaddled thus, but decided against it. They would have to fend for themselves in many ways now. This was merely one such.

Murphy wasted no time with the parting. He thanked Lieutenant Webber profusely while they were shaking hands. He was now already up on the seat alongside the driver. The wagon lurched forward as the driver started them down the pike southwest. The railway yard and station weren't far from the hospital, but the lieutenant had provided the cart for their departure to go smoothly. Patrick waved enthusiastically at the officer who had made their freedom a reality, then stopped abruptly when he realized he might bring unwanted attention.

They were at the railroad yard and off-loaded from the wagon a few minutes later. Things had happened so quickly since breakfast that the two young friends were still taking in their new circumstances with near-total disbelief. As they boarded the west-bound train they wondered: Could it actually be happening? Were they really free from this war?

\* \* \*

*Saturday, August 8, 1863. Late evening around a campfire in a sheltered site at the top of the pass between the Jocko River Valley and Hellgate, Idaho Territory.*

Rob poked at the wood of the fire, more of an idle distraction than to actually coax a larger flame. Victor and Tanehee sat positioned in such a way that the three of them made a large triangle surrounding the glowing embers. Rob was hoping that his conclusions regarding the threesome following them were correct. Otherwise his sending Walters, Wilson and Oce-asay ahead for repair parts for the wagon could be a mistake. He was confident in his plan, but was well aware that even the best plans fail in the face of unforeseen events.

When the three BMI operatives stepped suddenly from the underbrush with their guns drawn, Tanehee twitched slightly and Victor raised his head to better see his attackers. The leader of the armed intruders announced, "Hands up! No fast moves! We'll shoot if we have to!"

While raising his hands slowly above his head, Rob nearly sighed with relief. "No need for the guns, John. We won't give ya any trouble. Why not sit down an' join us?" He was trying to hide his grin, though mostly failing in that effort.

"Rob Finn! Is it really you? I thought you were still in Chicago!" The surprise in the man's voice was apparent to all. "And . . . how did you know it was me?" John Babcock was caught totally off-guard, a rarity in itself. Babcock was an intelligence operative when the two men had known one another. Only a year earlier, both men were employed by the Pinkerton Agency in Chicago.

Babcock started to answer his own question. "Ah, yes. Those famous Longshot eyes. You spotted me while we've been following you."

"More than once this past week, John, an' before that in Bannack." Rob's frank and unassuming delivery helped soothe the wounded pride of the other man. "Ah'd consider it a favor if you 'n' yer men would put away yer guns."

Babcock paused for a moment before replying, "I'm truly sorry to disappoint, old friend, but I'm going to have to place you under arrest until I get some questions answered." Babcock seemed to genuinely regret the demands of his job.

"Ah sure wish our traveling companions were here." Rob announced this pre-arranged signal in a much-louder-than-usual voice, which was not quite a shout.

Without making a sound, Walters, Wilson, and Oce-asay were suddenly standing, one each, behind the Bureau of Military Intelligence operatives. Each of the new arrivals held a double-barreled coach shotgun into the back of one BMI man–whose pistols were lowered to the ground in unison before another word was spoken.

Rob felt no urge to gloat, but could not resist acknowledging the irony of the moment. "Once again great minds think alike, John. But it seems it's us that'll be placing you under arrest. We also have some questions." With a nod of Rob's head, Victor took Oce-asay's place behind one of the BMI men and Oce-asay handed off his shotgun to the chief. The young warrior then proceeded to bind the wrists of the BMI men behind their backs and escort them to seated positions around the fire. He then built up the fire so all the faces surrounding it could be plainly seen.

Throughout the remainder of the night, Rob and Lonnie took turns questioning the three bound men to learn what they knew about Confederate operatives in the mining district, the Treasury Department agents, the gold shipments from Bannack, what their BMI orders were, and why they'd been following the Pinkerton group. Wilson and Oce-asay took turns watching the BMI men with the two Pinkerton agents. In this way, these four men plus Victor and Tanehee were able to rotate sleep shifts. This method also ensured their captives didn't sleep at all.

In the morning, the captors made sure their prisoners were well fed and watered, as they did the horses. Also like the horses, they provided them no coffee. Victor was off collecting a few important medicinal plants he had seen as they passed by on their way north a week earlier. Oce-asay and Tanehee watched over the bound BMI men and kept them awake while Rob, Lonnie, and Wilson re-installed the wagon wheel on its axle.

Observing that it was the same wheel that had been removed the previous afternoon and that no replacement parts were used in the process, Babcock correctly surmised, "So that was all just a ruse? There's nothing wrong with the wagon?"

Rob smiled and said, "We needed t' bring ya in for a closer look, John. We couldn't have ya followin' us all over creation, now, could we?"

"But I heard you send the other three for parts." Babcock stopped himself in mid-thought and shook his head in self-disgust. "I'll never hear the end of this."

"Don't let it worry ya too much. There may be a way out of this for all of us yet." Rob's answer offered a hint of hope to the dejected men seated on the ground. Their growing fatigue was obvious, especially when one of them toppled over after dozing off in his sitting position. Tanehee brought him back upright with a strong grip on his shoulder, then gave him a gentle prod with her moccasin-covered toe.

\* \* \*

*Monday, August 10, 1863. Early afternoon. About five miles west of St. Louis, on a freight wagon headed to Denver.*

The two passengers in the west-bound freighter were incredulous at their good fortune these past several days. Not only had their passage from Gettysburg to St. Louis gone quickly, but Billy had no pain nor blood loss from his wounds. When Patrick changed Billy's bandages at a stop in southern Indiana, he saw good new scar tissue covering all of that area where Billy's right shoulder had been. And the fingers of his left hand were pink, without deformity. Billy was able to squeeze Patrick's hand convincingly enough to prove there was no permanent nerve nor muscle damage there.

Billy suggested that Patrick need not apply new wrappings and Patrick was tempted to agree. Recalling the worst that might happen should any of Billy's wounds re-open or become infected, Patrick wisely insisted on applying them.

"It's only two more days, three at the most, Billy. Then if everything is still good, we'll leave them off. Be patient. I don't mind helpin' ya."

Their military travel vouchers ended with their steamboat crossing of the Mississippi River when they landed on the St. Louis side, in the state of Missouri. It was then that heaven seemed to especially smile upon these two lads from opposing armies. As they were casting about, racking their brains as to how they might get out of Missouri and into the western territories, Billy saw the Heinz Freighting Company sign painted in huge letters on a broadside of a building fronting the river docks. When he pointed it out to Patrick, they immediately started walking to the large, open loading-dock door below the sign. The short stairway up to the dock platform was an easy climb, even for Billy's challenged sense of balance.

The men loading a wagon with sacks of grain did not stop their work to answer Patrick's inquiry. One of them merely grunted, "Talk to the boss," as he jerked a thumb over his shoulder in the direction of a small, windowed room, with an "Office" sign attached to it. Murphy and Adams shuffled quickly out of the way of the workers and stood for a moment outside the open door into the small office. Patrick announced their presence with a loud rap to the doorframe.

The blonde-haired head that rose up from his ledgers in response to Patrick's knock revealed an intelligent face with caring eyes and a mouth that wanted to smile. While not elderly by any means, he was senior in age to the pair before him. He instantly took in the details of their dress, and Billy's obviously wounded condition, then stood up in order to come around to the front of his desk. He extended his right hand toward Patrick, (realizing politely without comment the futility of trying to shake Billy's), and introduced himself, "Heinz. Jeffery Heinz, gentlemen. What might I be able to do for you fine fellas?"

As quickly and plainly as they were able, Patrick and Billy explained their circumstances, their parole requirement that they leave the States, and their current plight of not having any means of travel, other than shanks mare. Heinz correctly surmised that they were without funds or any means to provide for themselves, and felt moved to help. But he needed to assure himself first that these two were not merely practiced beggars, (or worse),with a new twist to an old trade. He asked his few questions being careful to remain respectful toward the two strange young men in his place of business.

Patrick brought forth his signed parole document as proof of his claim; Heinz read it overly carefully before handing it back to the young Irishman, who had so recently been a Confederate corporal. Billy was still wearing his Union blue sack-coat with the right sleeve pinned closed and behind. Jeffery Heinz looked into each of the two pairs of honest, hopeful eyes standing before him and pronounced his decision, "You're in luck today, lads. I think we can help each other. Would you care to join me for a quick bite to eat?"

During their meal together, Jeff Heinz learned how each soldier had come by his injuries, their present state of prognosis and recovery, and that Adams was accompanying Murphy out of a sense of friendship. Heinz guessed at another motive being the fear of rejection at home, but said nothing. He had observed closely, (and he hoped surreptitiously), as Murphy fed Adams and helped him clean up during and after his meal. Quite unusual to see such a strong bond between erstwhile mortal enemies, Heinz thought.

But the two had convinced him of their sincerity, so he made his offer. "If the two of you would ride along with my driver to help keep an eye on things and protect the cargo, he'll take you to Denver. Depending on business prospects, he might even carry you further west–that decision will be his when it's time to leave Denver. I can't pay you anything other than to feed you along the way. There's just not enough profit in it." The further truth was that they were not really needed for the trip. Again, respect and a sense of charity caused him to keep that last detail to himself.

The excitement and joy in their expressions would have been more than enough acceptance for Heinz, but the young men also voiced their eager and grateful agreement to his proposal. Nearly an afterthought, Heinz said, "We'd probably best have a good look at Billy's healing before you go. You did say the wrappings were due to come off today?" Heinz managed to keep his tone one of polite and businesslike encouragement. He really did want to help this duo reach their destination.

Patrick carefully unwound the wrappings from around Billy's upper body in the modest confines of the freight company's small office. They were all relieved and pleased to see the clean pink scar tissue and to watch Adams' use of his now unfettered left hand and arm. He

flexed the fingers and thumb of the hand and pumped his forearm and upper arm to exercise them and the elbow. Finally he stretched long and hard before putting on one of his new shirts having just the left sleeve. Patrick helped him straighten and button it, while saying, "You'll get the hang of this in no time, Billy."

A happy young Billy agreed, "You bet I will, pard!"

Heinz was gratified by what he had witnessed and his smile attested to his feeling of goodwill. "You fellas best be getting on the wagon before Jenks drives off without you. He's not one to be kept waiting. And remember, he's the boss for this trip!"

Jenkins was among the best teamsters the Heinz family had ever employed. A burly Welshman, he was even-tempered, did not abuse his draft animals, delivered his loads reliably and on time. He kept to himself, didn't swear often and only rarely drank beer. The man looked over his shoulder at his two young "helpers" and said, "Let's go. Daylight's a'wastin'!"

Billy stepped forward and awkwardly clasped his left hand firmly into Heinz' offered right and shook it. "I can't thank you enough for the chance you've given us, Mr. Heinz! You won't be sorry, I promise that for both of us!" His smile was big enough to make Heinz certain he had done the right thing.

Having shaken hands with Heinz a few moments earlier, Murphy climbed aboard and helped Adams aboard while calling out, "He's right, Mr. Heinz. We won't let you down. Thanks for everything."

Heinz responded, "Take care of yourselves and my cargo. And mind whatever Jenks tells you to do!" His grin showed that his farewell contained hope for the success of the venture and those on it.

Jenks' whip cracked above the lead mules' heads as his snap of the leads reached their harness. His yell of "High-on!" was unneeded to get them started. Not only were his hand-picked mules well trained, they had been anxious to get on the road since before the wagon was finished loading nearly an hour earlier. The teamster's traveling companions continued to wave farewell to Heinz, who did likewise, until he finally turned back through the loading-dock entrance to rejoin his bookwork.

The tough old mule-skinner, (which term Jenkins hated), started his team of six sturdy mules off with a surprisingly brisk pace–surprising to those not yet familiar with the condition of the man and his beasts. And the Linstroth wagon he was driving was, for him, as the manufacturer's slogan suggested, "The Pride of St. Louis". A wide , firm, and straight roadway with no hills virtually guaranteed they would make 25 miles or more each full day of travel.

Among the many things that Jenkins liked about hauling for the Heinz family was the fact that they never over-loaded their shipments. Unbeknownst to the young men along with him, Mr. Heinz had ordered the removal of nearly three hundred pounds of goods from the wagon, thus lightening the load to better accommodate their travel aboard the wagon. As far as Jenks was concerned, that was no way to make money shipping freight across this wild country. But it was also not his decision, nor his problem, so he kept his thoughts about it to himself.

With the environs of St. Louis safely behind them, the spirits of the two former soldiers rose to a high state. They were two young men, on their way to the gold fields, having transportation and food, wide-open spaces before them, and that sense that their real adventures and fortunes in life were about to begin.

They truly had no idea what lay ahead ...

# CHAPTER FIVE

# Government Gold?

*Wednesday, August 12, 1863. Skinner's Saloon, Bannack, Idaho Territory, Noon.*

John Babcock leaned casually against the bar watching Treasury Agent Timothy Emry approach him from the entryway. Emry's eyes betrayed nervousness; they flitted around quickly, trying to take in all corners of the room at once.

"Glad you could make it, Emry," Babcock's cool greeting set just the tone he wanted for this meeting. "There's something in this for both of us."

Emry's face brightened and his eyebrows arched upward. The Bureau of Military Intelligence operative's comment piqued his interest. He'd had no idea what the man wanted from him, and the messenger, John Wilson, had been unable to provide any information.

Being it was a typically hot August day, both men quenched their thirsts with cold beer. Babcock paid (in gold dust, per Skinner's saloon policy) since he had invited the other to join him here. They took their glass steins from the bar and crossed to an empty table near the back of the room.

Still showing interest in the meeting's purpose, Emry asked, "What's on your mind, Babcock? I'm a busy man, not that I mind helping out a fellow government operative ... if I can."

Babcock moved carefully while placing a filled leather poke on the table, then setting two small gold ingots beside it. He had seated himself and placed the objects in such a way that Skinner would not be able to see them from behind the bar. Then he said, "That Pinkerton agent, Finn, says he knows where the road agents are hiding their gold. Says he thinks this sheriff, Plummer, may be behind the whole thing. Thinks Plummer's gang may have killed your partner, Daniels. Says he's found the body." Finished with his message, Babcock squared his shoulders and sat up straight in his chair. He watched Emry closely for any signs of anger, fear, or nervousness the man might give. Babcock would later attest that he had seen all three emotions present when the dapper Treasury man blurted, "Where?! Where did he find the gold?! Where is Daniels' body?!" His excited exclamations came much more in the form of demands than questions, and his voice had become unnaturally loud.

"Quiet down, Skinner doesn't need to know about this," Babcock said calmly. "They're evidently close together over near to the Alder Gulch diggings. Finn wants me to meet him where the Stinking Water River meets the Beaverhead at sunset on Friday. He's going to show me the body and the gold stash. As a fellow government operative, I thought you might like to be there. I don't trust these private investigators. Too easy for them to put something aside for themselves, if you know what I mean. I used to be one of 'em, you know," he chuckled.

"Are you saying we could arrest Finn?" Emry seemed incredulous.

"If the situation calls for it, we can. We'll do whatever it takes. We Federal officers need to stick together out in the wilds of the western territories. It's dangerous out here what with the wild Indians, wild animals, gold thieves, and such." Babcock added a conspiratorial grin to punctuate the end of his list.

"Yeah. You can say that again. Okay. Count me in. Where and when do I meet up with you?"

Following Emry's question, Babcock proceeded to fill him in on the details of the planned outing. During the conversation, Babcock carefully palmed the gold ingots before replacing them in his pocket. He handled the leather poke full of gold dust with similar care. Once the items were out of sight again, he relaxed slightly.

Their business concluded, they stood up to leave the saloon. Babcock added one comment in low voice, "Don't forget to bring a gun, Emry; you might need it." This last instruction was calculated to increase Emry's confidence that he and Babcock were partners in this enterprise, and

Rob Finn was the odd man out.

Emry rode his horse away from the stable on the eastern track out of Bannack, rather than taking the wagon road north to Alder Gulch. The eyes watching his eastward progress were not surprised by this fact; they merely noted his course and plotted where best to next intercept him.

Lonnie Walters had no difficulty shadowing Emry after the Treasury agent left Bannack. Emry lead him straight to a sheltered ravine not far off the trail he had taken out of town. It wasn't ten miles from the eastern edge of the diggings there. Once dismounted, Emry ducked behind a large boulder. Moments later, he stood, holding a gold ingot up into the sunlight and smiling. Then, looking furtively around, Emry bent back down behind the boulder. He shortly remounted his horse and again headed east.

When certain that Emry was gone and no one else was watching, Lonnie exited his hiding place and went into the ravine, there to search around behind the boulder. He soon found the large stash of gold which he was expecting.

After Lonnie described the hidden location to Rob, the two Pinkertons decided it would be best to leave the stash hidden in place for the time being. They did not share the location with anyone yet. But since the location was known to them, they could proceed with the other elements of Rob's plan. They talked with John Wilson, Victor and Oce-asay and later met with Babcock and his two fellow BMI operatives to finalize how they planned to trap Emry (and any others involved) on Friday evening.

Finn and Walters debated whether it would be best to have Plummer along for Friday's event, since Henry was the officially elected sheriff for the mining districts. They finally decided to inform Plummer of their plan, minus some of the details, and to invite him to the "party" as the local representative of law. Plummer declined the invitation due to his need to keep a watchful eye over his new bride and his own gold claims in Bannack, which were beginning to "pan out".

What turned out to be a lucky break for the Pinkertons had occured while they were at Fort Connah. A Salish hunting party from Victor's village had come across the Sioux encampment in a remote gully near the Alder Gulch diggings. Things remained peaceful during the encounter and a young member of the Sioux party even bragged about having killed one of the white men plundering the country. The warrior was very young, and quite proud that he had killed the designated enemy by himself, with a single blow from his war club. He had kept the odd-looking round hat from his dead opponent as a prize. The Salish group listened carefully, noting the location of the Sioux camp and details of the dead man's hat they were shown. When hearing the description of the hat during their days in the Salish village outside Fort Owen, Rob, Lonnie and John Wilson were all certain it matched one that Daniels had worn.

Rob found himself wishing that Bannack had its own telegraph office. He would have liked to send a message to his Chicago office to advise the current circumstances. Even more, he would have liked to send a telegram to Catherine who had been in his thoughts these past several days. And yes, he would have sent a telegram to Maggie, his recent bride, to offer her some comfort and encouragement in her present condition. But since there was no telegraph available, and since the only reliable messenger around, John Wilson, was occupied by this present mission, he had no means to get a message to family members just then. Realizing the futility of his circumstances, Rob did his best to put family and office matters out of his mind.

*  *  *

*Thursday, August 13, 1863. Early afternoon along the Beaverhead River, a few miles south of the rock formation after which it was named.*

Bricks and Roxie seemed to be enjoying the relaxed pace of their ride nearly as much as were Rob and Lonnie. The two men had gone over the relevant facts of the case as it now unfolded before them. No longer was there any doubt about who was really behind the gold shipment robberies, nor about who was responsible for the death of the Treasury agent, Daniels. And they had evidence needed for both the robberies and the murder.

When they passed the place where Oce-asay had secured his sister's body in the cottonwood tree the previous November, they were silent for a while. The body was no longer in the tree. They'd heard about the sad ceremony which took place in early spring when the entire village made the journey to retrieve Jodenaha's body and put it in a more permanent place, closer to the village where she had lived.

It was not much further along that they recognized the place of last fall's grizzly bear attack and the area they had camped during Rob's treatment and recuperation. Rob halted Bricks, sat up straight in the saddle and drew a deep breath. "At the time, Lonnie, Ah didn't realize how much ya went through t' save my life. Brave as it was on your part, killing that bear was only the beginning of it, from what Ah have come t' know an' what Ah'm now able to recall." He let out a deep sigh. "Ah know Ah've thanked ya already. Ya need t' know Ah'll never be able t' thank ya enough."

"I'm plenty happy things turned out the way they did, Rob. I did what I could, but if Victor hadn't shown up when he did, I don't believe you would have lived. Not in your right mind, anyway. And for the record, you're very welcome. I'd do it all again if need be." There was no eye contact between them for a while as they silently resumed their ride north and east. Sometimes men don't want other men to see their eyes.

Victor and Oce-asay were a half day's ride ahead of them with John Wilson and the wagon bearing Michel Ogden's gold, headed to a predetermined spot in the Stinking Water River valley near to its confluence with the Beaverhead River. Once there, they would secure the wagon nearby out of sight. They would hide their horses nearby, as well, and the men would be in hiding to await the approach of their Pinkerton friends. Or others, for that matter.

Rejoined as a team that evening, Rob, Lonnie, Victor, Oce-asay and John Wilson had plenty to do prior to the next evening's planned rendezvous. Unloading the gold from the wagon, safely hiding it, then finding and securing locations to picket the horses, get the wagon out of sight, and provide cover for those who would be hidden when their guests arrived would consume plenty of time. In addition, since they were just off the trail between Bannack and Alder Gulch, they needed to hide each time passers-by were spotted  John Wilson proved to be additionally helpful in being able to translate freely between Salish and English. Though Victor was somewhat fluent in English, John's explanations back-and-forth to Oce-asay and to Victor (though required less often) assured their teamwork and trust would not be eroded by misunderstandings.

They made a simple trail-side camp that night and slept around a small campfire they had made. Taking turns at sentry duty made good sense; even though they had removed the Ogden gold from the wagon. For tonight, they were merely traveling companions camped on their way between the two most active gold-digging sites in the entire territory. There was certainly nothing in that appearance to raise any suspicions.

* * *

*Friday, August 14, 1863. A campsite on the Stinking Water River just upstream from its confluence with the Beaverhead.*

Shortly before dawn, Oce-asay wakened Rob by shaking the man's shoulder. There was a group of Indians, probably ten or more, that had approached to within one hundred fifty yards of their wagon and campsite. It was unclear what their intentions might be, so Oce-asay woke Rob and Wilson; Wilson and Oce-asay then proceded to wake the others.

All five of the companions were fully awake on the instant. Rob, standing next to Victor, shielded his eyes from the pre-dawn light growing in the east, attempting to see clearly in that direction. Oce-asay had pointed out a small hill with a large rock formation on its north side as being the present hiding place of the raiding Indians. The fact that Rob made no attempt to bring his long-range Sharps rifle to bear on the potential enemies was not lost on Victor.

As the senior of the two Salish tribesmen present, Victor called out in a clear, loud voice, speaking in his Salish tongue. There was no immediate response from the rock formation. Lonnie and Wilson wondered if it had been a false alarm. Victor and Rob had greater trust in Oce-asay's skills and were thus certain that danger lurked there.

Victor then switched his calling out to English, simply asking, "Who are you, my brothers? What do you need?" Again his words were met with silence while all five sets of eyes strained to detect any movement.

After what seemed like many minutes, (which was more likely a matter of seconds), a reply reached their ears. "Need food ... medicine. Man bad sick." A moment later, a tall Sioux brave stepped from behind the rock formation into plain sight. His hands were empty, and, other than a knife in his sash, he had no weapons on his person.

Victor started immediately to cross the gap between them, picking up his medicine pouch from the back of the wagon as he went. Victor's strong, upright gait was impressive at anytime, but when his intent or purpose was urgent, he became like a being of legends. He somehow seemed taller, younger, and he certainly covered ground more quickly than other men his age. His stride quickly put him halfway across the distance. So quickly, in fact, that Rob, Lonnie and John were caught off guard, watching with open-mouthed wonder. None of them knew what to expect. Oce-asay had already grabbed up his lance from where he had earlier kept watch and was closing the distance between himself and Victor. If the white men knew nothing else about their Native companions, they knew they were men of action more than words.

Wilson and Walters each grabbed their short-barreled coach shotguns and took off after Rob. Rob had the Colt revolver holster on his hip, a pocket pistol in his vest, and a knife hidden in his boot. He did not pause to take any of the long guns available to him.

Before Victor and Oce-asay reached the lone Sioux brave, three more men appeared from behind the outcropping. Two were supporting the third between them. The man between them looked to be in rough shape, unconscious or worse. As the two groups came nearer each other, more Sioux warriors stepped out into view. These were armed with bows, though none had arrows fitted to them. They had a fearsome look to them, yet none seemed menacing or threatening at the moment.

The two helpers laid the injured man on the ground. Victor was immediately kneeling alongside, examining the patient with concern in his experienced eyes. The patient was young; he was noticeably younger-looking than his companion braves. His eyes were mostly closed (though the lids fluttered at times) and his breathing was shallow.

The right leg below the knee was swollen to twice normal size. Nearly the entire leg had turned a dark purple; swelling also showed above the knee all the way to the hip. Lonnie had already joined Victor, kneeling on the opposite side of the downed man. A brief and knowing look passed between them.

The sun's rise was rapid in this country and the growing light made plain the source of the problem. Two swollen puncture wounds on the young Sioux's bared right ankle looked angry and threatening. Two more sets of bite wounds were visible, one on each of the patient's wrists. These showed no swelling nor discoloration, indicating the likelihood that no venom entered those sites.

The first Sioux to hail Finn's group threw down the recently severed tail of a rattlesnake. He blurted out, "Enapay walk on snake–snake bite Enapay."

Victor asked the man three questions in the Lakota tongue, each containing only few words. The Sioux leader answered, also with few words. All listening heard the names 'Bannack' and 'Plummer'. Wilson caught some of rest of the meaning, but not enough to translate. Victor informed the others, "Bite two nights ago, young man away from camp. Leg dark, swelling when he get back. Friends suck out poison, young man collapse. They go to Bannack, find friend Plummer."

Finn, Walters, and Wilson were surprised to learn of this connection. Then a thought occurred to Rob, one which he was surprised not to have thought of before.

These were the same Sioux Indians he and Wilson had seen riding with Emry several weeks before just a few miles outside Bannack. He looked at Wilson, about to say something when a look of knowing recognition crossed Wilson's face. He, too had made the connection. Rob wondered if there were a further connection, one between Emry and Plummer.

"Things are about to get real interesting." Rob's comment summed up what both he and Wilson were thinking.

Victor and Lonnie were working on the fallen young Sioux, concern showing on their sweat-soaked faces. Despite the early hour, the two healers had been exerting themselves to help the sick young man who lay, fighting for his life, as the skilled hands and minds tended him as best they could. With the venom so advanced, applying a tourniquet and removing the leg was out of the question. Both caregivers knew there was little hope of their patient surviving; he was too far gone when they first saw him. Victor passed herbal combinations to Lonnie, either to be brewed into teas or blended with small quantities of resin and wrapped in hot wet cloths as poultices.

Making the patient more comfortable was the only realistic goal left to them. The combined, steady efforts of two experienced, dedicated healers seemed to finally have the desired effect. The patient's eyes opened and he breathed more deeply. Looking around, the young Sioux looked at their leader and motioned with a finger, almost imperceptibly. The older Sioux leaned closer to the young man so that his ear was near Enapay's mouth.

A smile appeared on the elder's face but soon changed to one of puzzlement and finally sorrow. He looked up from the young warrior and asked Victor, "He live?"

Victor's deep-set eyes answered in such a way that no word was needed. The Sioux leader, whose name was Mankato, allowed his shoulders to sag and took a deep breath. This was followed by a long sigh. Mankato's countenance became one of complete sadness. Enapay was his youngest son. A sudden, unnatural outrush of air left Enapay's mouth, his eyes were opened wide, his body shuddered and became still. He was dead.

It was a tense moment as the two groups of men, gathered on opposite sides of the dead body, regarded one another. Eleven Sioux warriors stood across from the three US citizens and their two Salish escorts. Victor's and Lonnie's best efforts and ministrations had failed to save Enapay's life. Now what?

* * *

*Friday, August 14, 1863. Mid-morning, north of the confluence of the Stinking Water River (also known as the Ruby River)*

Before parting from the Pinkerton group, the Sioux Indians explained how Emry recruited them, their roles in the robberies, two other killings, and finally, the Daniels murder. As it turned out, Enapay was the young warrior who had boldly bashed in Daniels' skull with a single fatal blow from his war club, later bragging to a Salish hunting party passing through. Since Enapay was now dead as well, there was no need for pursuing any punishment for that act, other than to include in the record that Emry had ordered the killing.

Emry had promised the Sioux immunity from prosecution, plenty of food, and to help them with any trouble that came up. He told them he was a chief with the Big Government in Washington. He had promised to check in with them no less often than every other day. Mankato had waited an entire extra day for Emry to show up, a day they could have been seeking help for Enapay. They felt their loyalty in following Emry's instructions had been betrayed and it cost Enapay's life.

Finn and Babcock further learned that Emry had used the name of Henry Plummer as his own, teaching the Sioux tribesmen to refer to him thusly as part of the overall ruse. It worked exceptionally well due to the physical similarities between Plummer and Emry, especially with those that did not know either man well.

The Sioux warriors were sickened at the way Emry abandoned them after all his promises. Were it not for their keen desire to return to their tribal lands, they would gladly have done whatever they could to repay his behaviors.

All things considered, especially the grievous wrongs committed by the US and Minnesota State governments against the Sioux tribe, Finn, Walters and Babcock all agreed it would be unjust to bring these men in for questioning or prosecution. They knew it would be impossible for them to get a fair trial and doubted that Emry's conscience would force him to tell the truth of his involvement with them, even under oath. Perhaps especially not while under oath.

They held a lengthy meeting with all present participating. John Wilson's translating was again a great help to the process. The strong positive relationship between the Pinkertons, Wilson, and the two Salish men carried much weight as the Sioux considered the words exchanged and their options. Eleven remaining Sioux warriors were unanimous in wanting to return to their tribe. Recent events during their raiding ventures for Emry had dulled their desire for revenge. Enapay's unfortunate death, and the manner of it (which they took as a spirit sign) ended any remaining thoughts of avenging the Federal massacre of their thirty-eight dead brothers. As a point of reference, by their reckoning, they had participated in the killing of eighteen white miners–less than half what the governments had inflicted upon their people.

Mankato, the Sioux leader, made clear his band's eagerness to leave. They wanted no gold. They wanted to be riding back east as soon as possible. They had plenty of their own provisions for the journey, but as a token of goodwill and friendship, accepted small sacks of sugar and flour, together with a roll of pemmican. In exchange, they insisted on giving Lonnie and Victor each an elaborate beaded headband for their services trying to save Enapay.

Parting words were brief. The Sioux mounted their ponies and, together with the pony carrying the fur-wrapped body of Enapay being led by Mankato, rode away to the east without further ado.

Victor and Oce-asay were again pleased by the respectful, courteous behavior Finn, Walters, and Wilson had shown toward the Sioux. Such observations further supported their belief that they were trusting good men.

* * *

*Friday, August 14, 1863. Just before sunset on a patch of ground within easy sight of the Beaverhead and Stinking Water (Ruby) River confluence.*

Rob stood watching as Emry rode up to his position, arriving from the West as expected. Bricks was tethered loosely to a large sagebrush; their backs to the small hill with the rock outcropping where so much had taken place earlier in the day. John Babcock and his two assistants rode alongside Emry.

While the arriving horsemen were yet approaching, Rob called out loudly, "Hello, Babcock. Hello, Emry.

Didn't expect to see you here." An element of surprise carried in his words to Babcock.

"Life's full of surprises, Finn. You should know that by now," was Babcock's casual reply.

The four newcomers reined in, dismounted and tethered their horses before joining Rob at the small fire where he stood. Everyone was armed with holstered pistols, even Emry. Rob noted this change in the Treasury man's get up. He had never seen Emry carry nor handle a gun.

Babcock took a position across the fire pit from Rob while his three companions arrayed themselves to his left side. No one touched a weapon, nor moved their hands nearer to doing so. "Let's get to this evening's business, shall we, friend?" Babcock's words and easy manner betrayed no sign of malice.

When Emry spoke in his high-pitched nasal voice, his words dripped with contempt. "Show us Plummer's stash of gold, Finn, so we can be done with this matter. That gold belongs to the US Government, and I aim to take possession of it here and now!" He shook with excitement at his own utterance.

"Hang on a minute, Emry. Let's not get ahead of ourselves, shall we? We haven't seen any gold yet. Let's see the gold and the body first. There's plenty of time for taking possession. Nobody's going anywhere. Right, Finn?" Babcock's wink at Rob was just discernible in the gathering shadows. Being the night of August's new moon assured it would be as dark as could be. The clear night sky would allow for plenty of starshine during their proceedings, however.

"Not far, Babcock, that's for sure. We're right close t' both the gold stash an' Daniels' body, both within easy walking distance. This won't take long. We can leave the horses here for now. Follow me an' watch your step." Rob turned about and started walking toward the hills where they met the base of the valley. His objective was a narrow ravine there, where a seasonal watercourse had carved deep into the hillside. There was no water flowing at this time of year. As he passed by the rock outcropping, Rob was careful not to turn his head even slightly in that direction.

Shadows continued to stretch long as they crossed the valley. Rob was walking at a pace slower than his usual and making a show of using great care to pick his footfalls. By the time they reached the opening of the ravine, the sun had set completely and darkness engulfed them. Starlight was just sufficient for them to make out shapes and vague shadows. They slowed more when they entered the ravine, where the darkness was more complete.

Coyotes yapping from ahead and above them startled Emry and the BMI trio momentarily. They paused, then resumed the march immediately. It was only coyotes, after all. Nothing to worry about.

Ahead of the startled foursome, Rob Finn had begun to climb the side-wall of the ravine. He continued about twenty feet upward before stopping. "This is it, Babcock. This is where the stolen gold is buried."

Emry scrambled past the others, climbing to the place where Rob stood. "Where?" he demanded, "Let's see this hoard of gold!"

Rob leaned forward, removed a carefully stacked cairn of rocks from the uphill side of a larger boulder, and started pulling out the mud-stained leather pouches of Odgen's trove of gold. He set them carefully on top of the boulder where they could be seen in the starlight.

Emry took a step forward, picked up the pouch nearest him and held it to his eyes for closer examination. "That's not ...", he stopped himself before finishing his exclamation.

"Not what?" Finn queried the smaller man.

"Just not, uh ... what I expected to see ... I guess."

"Oh. Ah see," Rob commented. "What were ya expecting?" He pressed the question gently but firmly toward the other.

"Let it be, Finn! It's not your business!" Emry shouted. "This is a Federal matter, so Babcock and I will be handling things from here out. I'm taking possession of this stash in the name of the US Government. But thanks for showing us the ... uh thieves' stash." Emry's thanks sounded sincere, for indeed it was. Emry estimated to himself that his net worth in gold had more than doubled in one evening's work.

A few pebbles slid down from above where Finn and Emry stood perched on the side of the ravine. This slide was followed by bouncing rocks, still small enough not to cause real concern. What followed next in the dim starlight caused Emry to suck his breath in quickly. Most derby or bowler hats were black; brown hats were the exception. Light gray hatbands were rarely seen. Sitting upright on its brim was a brown derby hat with a light gray band; the exact combination that Daniels had worn. This bit of damning evidence had come to rest on the ground at Emry's feet, the brim touching his boot toe.

Emry froze while panic took hold of his features. He pulled the holstered pistol and aimed it unsteadily at Rob. "What's going on here?!" he shrieked. "What's the meaning of this?!"

"It means that we've found ya out, Emry. You won't be taking any gold along where you're going. Jail is hardly good enough for the likes of you. Stealing is bad enough, but you've murdered your innocent partner."

Emry shouted, " Innocent! Daniels wasn't innocent. He was in on ..." he cut himself short, realizing the folly of his argument. "Never mind! I'll be taking this gold with me, anyway, Finn. Right, Babcock?"

The sound of multiple gun hammers being cocked in rapid succession from above, below, and around the small gathering interrupted the conversation.

" 'fraid not, Emry. It's like you said a moment ago. This all belongs to the US Government. But thanks for thinking of me ... pardner."

\* \* \*

*Wednesday, August 19, 1863. At a remote campsite in a canyon adjacent to the Hell's Canyon Creek drainage.*

Aware of how capricious and unpredictable miners' courts and territorial justice could be, Babcock and Finn had agreed before conducting their combined operation against Emry that they would remove whatever gold turned up, including Ogden's trove (though that was a separate, private matter), away from the mining district. Their intention was to head south to Salt Lake City, there to turn Emry over to the Federal marshall to await trial. Beyond that, they thought they could ride along together to Denver, helping each other with guarding the gold being transported. They expected that, by the time they reached Denver, there would be telegraphed orders for them in response to their wired reports they would send from Salt Lake City. Nothing had been decided upon past arriving together in Denver.

For now, it would take several days to gather their forces, load another wagon with Emry's stash of gold on Grasshopper Creek, then rejoin forces for their travel to

Salt Lake City. Meanwhile, for "trust and safekeeping", Crisman's wagon laden with the Ogden trove was with the Babcock team.

During those days following their discovery and capture of Emry, Babcock and his crew, with the addition of Oce-asay and John Wilson, escorted Emry to a pre-selected and secluded campsite several miles north of the spot where they had trapped and apprehended him. He was now shackled hand and foot to keep him from attempting an escape. Managing Emry, his daily needs, and transportation was tedious work that kept the three BMI operatives on edge. They were tempted several times to remove his shackles so that he could tend to himself without their assistance, especially for matters of personal hygiene.

One of Babcock's men, Pete Doyle by name, finally lost his patience with Emry's whining and wheedling. Taking matters into his own hands, Doyle unlocked Emry's shackles after extracting his promise not to "attempt any escape or other shenanigans." Speaking the words of the promise lasted longer than the keeping of it. While Doyle bent over to finish unlocking the mechanism securing Emry's ankles, Emry clubbed him on the back of the head with a rock he had palmed. Since the nature of their departure from the other men at camp was prompted by "personal need" and privacy, the activity took place out of their sight and hearing.

* * *

*Wednesday, August 19, 1863. Bannack, Idaho Territory.*

Things in Bannack had been mostly quiet. Miners mined, merchants traded with their customers, teamsters came and went. Then, on August 19th, two men sharing ownership in a claim got into an altercation. Peter Horen shot his partner John Keeley at the height of their disagreement. The wound proved to be fatal. Henry Plummer arrested and jailed Horen to await the outcome of the trial.

# CHAPTER SIX

# Lawless Men And Truth

*Thursday, August 20, 1863. Late afternoon on level ground approaching a ford of Little Blue River, outside the town of Independence, Missouri.*

Owing to rain squalls at several points along the way, the Heinz Company freight wagon driven by Jenkins, carrying Patrick Murphy and Billy Adams, was behind schedule coming into the Kansas City environs. Jenkins fretted about the delays; he prided himself on being on time.

When four riders with bandanas masking their faces emerged from a roadside clump of trees demanding they stop, Jenkins decided to test their resolve by popping his whip over the mules' heads and hollering "High-on" in a loud and excited voice, thus urging the animals to gallop, in direct opposition to the bandits' orders.

For his troubles, Jenkins received a bullet that grazed his head, rendering him unconscious and knocking him backward off the high seat into the bed of the wagon. Patrick grabbed the reins and drew back while calling out, "Whoa, whoa, there," repeatedly. The mules finally responded, stopping the wagon alongside the river.

Four masked marauders each held a pistol aimed at the occupants of the wagon, as they took positions cutting off any further attempt to get away. Patrick and Billy were not about to try any heroics, being unarmed and outnumbered as they found themselves. Jenkins' low groan signaled that he was still alive. He had landed on a pile of bags filled with seeds, preventing further injury. His head wound was bleeding freely, and he remained unconscious.

Patrick and Billy exchanged worried looks when one of the robbers called out, "What'r'ya hauling there, boys? Got any guns or grub?" Billy sat near where Jenkins landed and was trying to gently rouse the man. The speaker turned his attention to him and said, "Go ahead and look him over, Yank. Just don't try anything fancy, ya hear?" Next he turned toward Patrick and said, "How about it ... you carrying any guns? You got any food?"

Figuring their chances would be best if he told the truth, Patrick explained that there was a coach shotgun under the seat he was on, that what food stuffs they carried were sacks of flour and sugar and cases of tinned beans, tomatoes, carrots and oysters for wholesale trade. Other than that, they had such vittles as were along for their own consumption; mostly depleted. Kansas City was their planned place to restock their traveling supplies.

He added that he and Billy were war veterans; Billy with a medical discharge and himself with a parole requiring he travel west of the States. Since Kansas had achieved Statehood, this meant Patrick needed to get beyond its western border, into Colorado Territory, to meet the terms of his parole.

One of the other robbers dismounted and, while the rest kept their guns trained on Patrick and Billy, climbed up and removed the shotgun from beneath the freighter's high seat. He poked around further, looking for other weapons. Finished with his search, he called down to the other, "Only this coach gun, here, Cole. He was tellin' the truth."

"Bring it down with ya, Frank, if ya don't mind," the one named Cole answered. He then said, "I can see your friend gave his arm for the Union cause. What's your story? USA or CSA?"

"8th Virginia Infantry, Confederate," Patrick replied, wondering what would happen next. He was concerned about Jenkins' condition and could think of nothing to extricate them from the present situation.

"I was in the Missouri Militia, CSA for a while myself. Even been paroled a couple of times. That's all in the past now. We're done with governments and their armies. Listen, now. No need for any more shootin'. That driver hadn't tried to be a hero, he'd still be sittin' up on the bench. I just knicked him–don't think he's hurt too bad." Continuing on, Cole added, "We need to take a little flour and sugar off your hands; maybe some of them tinned goods. We got no grudge against any CSA soldier, so long as you keep tellin' us true. How'd you happen to be travelin' with this blue-belly?"

Patrick told the story of how both he and Billy had been wounded at Gettysburg, and that he became a volunteer hospital orderly after recovering substantially from his own concussion. He told how their friendship had formed during his weeks of providing orderly care for Billy, and finally, how when it became time for Patrick to be paroled, he asked for Billy to be discharged into his care. His sincerity convinced the robbers enough that they holstered their guns and lowered their bandanas.

Cole said, "Just keep your hands out in the open and don't make any quick moves. How's that driver seem to you? He gonna be alright?" His concern sounded genuine.

Patrick, mindful of the instruction that they move slowly, climbed over and down to the bed of the wagon to examine Jenkins. He found that the bullet had indeed merely grazed the man's head, high in the hairline, from front to back. It left a furrow in the scalp along which the flow of blood was already slowing and starting to congeal. Jenkins murmured and sat up when Patrick's hands were run across his head. The bullet did not penetrate the skull, thus leaving only the minor scalp wound. Jenkins would recover. Patrick informed the robbers of his diagnosis.

Cole, Frank, and their two companions directed their three captives to climb down off the wagon, which they did. Cole then walked them to a nearby grassy patch and directed them to sit down. The man seemed kindly, especially for one in his line of work. He surprised his three charges with the next words he spoke.

"We're not part of the Confederacy anymore, either. There's as many crooks trying to run the south as there are in the north. You said you're headed west–to the territories. Good. You're better off where there's no government tellin' ya what to think and do. We're on our way to California, got some business there. Where you boys headed?"

Patrick found Cole's use of the term 'boys' to be similar to the talk used by his CSA comrades in the 8th Virginia Infantry. Both Cole and Frank appeared to be about his same age; the other two robbers were definitely younger-looking, younger than Billy. Probably fifteen-year-olds, Patrick thought to himself.

"This load is meant for Denver, not that it's any of your business." Jenkins' headache didn't stop him from answering. "Maybe on to the gold fields after that. See how it goes, as they say." His mood toward his captor was less surly as he completed his answer. He had overheard the comments Cole had made to Patrick. Mostly he agreed with what that young man had said.

Patrick and Billy chimed in with comments about seeking their fortunes in the gold fields around Virginia City or Bannack. They couldn't return to the States until the war was over or until two years had passed, whichever came first, according to Patrick's parole document.

"Don't ever go back to the States. Stay out West and keep lookin' for gold. The folks runnin' the country are ruinin' it, and they don't give damn about the likes of you 'n' me. But for right now, you'd best stay this side of the Big Muddy for another day or two. There's some dangerous business about to take place just up ahead in Kansas. You don't want to be there for it. Take my advice. Wait for two days after we clear off. We mean you no harm and we're only gonna lighten your load by a little–just takin' what we need to get by for a couple days. We'll even leave your shotgun where you can see it when we go."

True to his word, the robbers finished taking what supplies they needed, unloaded Jenkins' coach gun and left it in plain sight across the Little Blue River, on the bank where the road slanted down to the ford. As the four men rode away west, Cole turned and gave a brief wave to the three men seated on the ground near the river.

"That's about as friendly a robbery as I've ever heard of," Jenkins' comment reflected the feelings of the group. "Glad that young feller's aim wasn't off. As it is, my head hurts something awful."

Patrick started a fire, gathered a few willow switches from the river bank and brewed tea to help ease Jenkins' pain. It wasn't late enough for darkness to set in, but due to Jenkins' recent wounding and the robber's instructions, they prepared to camp right there for the night.

They woke to a perfectly still, beautiful day with a clear blue sky and a bright sun rising in the east. During breakfast they discussed whether they should continue on or wait another day or longer as the robber had told them. Jenkins was anxious to continue on and insisted they were in no more danger doing so than they would be sitting at this riverside. Besides his greater age and experience, he was officially in charge of this expedition to Denver. The two younger men made no argument.

After sending a telegram to the Heinz Company in St. Louis informing them of the robbery, the threesome purchased eggs, bacon, and coffee from a grocery close to the Red Bridge crossing the Big Blue River in Independence. Their "friendly" robbers really hadn't taken much.

They were on the road early and made good time after passing the western edges of Kansas City in the new State, following along the road on the south side of the Kansas River. The entire day was pleasant and uneventful. Fine weather combined with a smooth and relatively flat road helped their spirits rise. The mules seemed glad of the change from the wetter, drearier passage they experienced crossing the State of Missouri. Jenkins had made this run to Denver with this same team of mules on numerous occasions, so was familiar with the road ahead.

Despite stopping in Independence and moving at slower speeds while there and in Kansas City, they had covered more than thirty miles on this Friday, August 21st. Jenkins was pleased with and proud of his mules and told his two passenger/helpers as much. They camped before the sun set in the western sky and had another balmy night for sleeping. Saturday morning, upon awaking before dawn, all three of the men sensed something was wrong.

The mules were restless and braying, there was more smoke in the air than their campfire could have produced. Was there a grassfire nearby? That would be nothing to take lightly.

Hurriedly dressing and attending to essential chores to get on the road, they opted to skip breakfast until after putting a few miles behind them. The smoke on the distant horizon was thickest where it rose in the sky ahead and slightly north.

Several miles further along, Jenkins let out with, "By God! That's Lawrence! Lawrence is burning!"

He immediately spurred his team to greater speed while concentrating on the clouds of smoke billowing up in the distance. Once recovered from the jostling caused by the wagon's sudden lurch forward, both Patrick and Billy kept their eyes riveted toward the source of the smoke. They expected to see flames flaring into the sky at any moment as they approached the town at their accelerated speed.

\* \* \*

In 1863, Lawrence, Kansas was home to some of the most heated debates and feelings about abolitionist and Free-State movements. Most people living in the growing city were opposed to slavery being allowed and the most fervent among them were commonly referred to as Jayhawkers. Within the ranks of those calling themselves thusly, were some radical men willing to carry their beliefs beyond discussion.

"Red Legs" was the term applied to those members of militias who carried out raids in Missouri against any who opposed their way of thinking. This nickname (which they and others applied to them) reflected the distinctive red leggings they wore over the lower portions of their trouser legs. There was no official recognition of these guerrilla groups; they acted independently of government troops even while modeling their uniforms and command structures after the army of their allegiance.

Main targets for their raids into Missouri were slave-holding farms and anyone bold enough to speak out against the Red Legs' particular brand of brutality. The Red Legs used Lawrence as one of their bases of operation, a headquarters of sorts. This was due to the fact that one of their main supporters and leaders, Senator James Lane, called Lawrence home. Lane had led some of the Missouri raids, none of which was less than atrocious in outcome. Red Legs were feared far and wide for their blood-thirsty tactics, especially when they went hunting their opponents in Missouri.

No less ruthless than their Kansas-based counterparts were the Missouri Bushwackers. By 1863, William Quantrill was nationally known as the leader of Quantrill's Raiders. Those that rode with Quantrill included a wide assortment of former Missouri State Militiamen, Confederate soldiers, and citizens who had fallen victim to the Union Army or renegade organizations such as the Red Legs. Riding with Quantrill during the Lawrence Raid were Bloody Bill Anderson, Cole Younger and Frank James. Younger and James each had a little brother along for the ride and to watch over.

\* \* \*

*Saturday, August 22, 1863. Late morning among the smoldering ruins of former downtown Lawrence, Kansas.*

"We should burn ALL the buildings!" Yelled the wild-haired, heavily-bearded man on horseback as he galloped forward, looking over his shoulder at an unmounted man with a neatly trimmed mustache and beard. The rider looked up in time to realize that he was nearly upon the slow-moving freight wagon as it pulled to a halt. "Watch where you're going, ya old coot!" These words were directed at Jenkins as the rider stood in his stirrups, drew his revolver, cracked Jenkins on the head with the barrel, and pulled his horse's head sharply to the left nearly causing the animal to stumble. But in the end, Bloody Bill Anderson had succeeded in venting his anger while avoiding a collision.

Jenks was not impressed by the athletic moves of his assailant. He was again head-over-heels into the wagon bed, landing upon the same sacks of seeds that had cushioned his fall less than two days earlier. Patrick and Billy moved as one to attend their friend. He was again unconscious. Having experienced a serious head wound himself, as well as attending many more while working as an orderly, Patrick said quietly, "Lost consciousness again. That's not good, especially at his age."

He was merely repeating what he had heard doctors at Gettysburg say. Nevertheless, his concern for the Welsh driver was genuine. What would happen if Jenks didn't regain full consciousness? Or worse? Patrick didn't like to consider either option.

A familiar voice from the sidewalk reached their ears. "I thought I told you boys to wait two days before following after us. Seems you ain't so good at following orders." There was no threat in the words nor the voice delivering them. Patrick and Billy whipped around to see the man they knew as Cole standing alongside the well-dressed and mustachioed stranger they had spotted earlier. Cole was smiling, if a little uneasily, when he spoke to the man near him, "They're harmless enough, sir. Gave us some rations and sent us on our way when last we met. Ain't that so, Virginia?"

Cole was obviously referring to Patrick's unit affiliation, so he answered back, "Yep. That's so."

It was only good fortune that the warm temperatures had caused Billy to finally shed his Union sack coat with its pinned-back sleeve. He was wearing a white cotton shirt which did nothing to hide his disfiguring wound. But his Union uniform was not present to indicate his affiliation with the north.

The other man calmly stated, "If you say so, Cole." Then he turned to Patrick and said," You'd best move this wagon off the main street before it gets commandeered." He turned, mounted his horse and rode off after his wild-haired associate.

"You know who that was?" Cole asked Patrick and Billy. "That was the one-and-only William Quantrill. He's not the bad man you might read about in the newspapers; none of us are." At that he laughed a short high-pitched bark. "Let's get you out of harm's way."

Cole Younger took hold the harness of the lead mule and clucked as he led the team up the street, turning onto the first side street they met. Patrick and Billy were amazed to see a number of bodies lying about on the streets and sidewalks as they passed. It looked like a war zone. Most, but not all, of the bodies were men. There were women and boys down, also.

Noting the direction their eyes were taking and the reactions on their faces, Younger commented aloud to those in the wagon, "War is a dirty, bloody business. It is the business of governments and bankers. Stay as far away from it as you can, for as long as you can, and you'll do alright." His words were heavy with feeling, especially for someone Cole's age.

Before they had traveled much further, Cole halted the mules' progress. Frank James stepped into the street leading two saddled horses, walking out from alongside one of the few unburnt structures yet standing, and asked, "How far ya takin' this bunch?"

Younger's reply was clear and loud enough to be heard by everyone in the vicinity. "Right here is where I'm leaving these friends of mine. They may stay in town awhile to patch up their companion; they may not. I don't care and it don't matter. It's none of my business. Besides, the rest of us have work to do. Quantrill's waitin' for us to join him just outside of town. We're headed to Texas. Bloody Bill has already gone on ahead, so Quantrill's gonna be in a hurry to get going. Slow pokes might just get left behind to greet the Red Legs. If that don't suit, ya'd best mount up and ride south."

Patrick looked around them at what was left of the town. He was wondering if Younger might have been hoping to address the two teenaged riders who had been with them at the river crossing two days before. They were nowhere to be seen, but several scruffy-looking men darted in and out of ruined buildings, busy with the work of plunder.

Cole's smile widened, and Frank actually showed a little smirk. Cole lowered his voice to normal speaking volume and addressed Patrick's unspoken question, "Our little brothers are waitin' for us outside of town. They're not old enough to get involved in man's work yet; not that they wouldn't like to ..."

Then he and Frank mounted their horses, turning in the direction both Anderson and Quantrill had taken so recently.

Younger turned back in the saddle again, made eye contact with Patrick and said, "Keep going west. Stay out of the way of governments and their wars. Good luck!" He tipped his hat and turned to the path ahead of him. Frank James, who had also turned in his saddle to face the wagon and its passengers, tipped his hat and smiled before turning to catch up to Cole.

A low moan emanating from the wagon bed returned Patrick and Billy to the reality that they had a wounded comrade to attend. Jenkins sat up by himself, wavered momentarily, then fell slowly back onto the seed sacks. When the two young veterans heard, "I'm gonna be sick," they quickly hoisted him up by the shoulders in time for him to vomit over the side of the wagon.

Though Patrick recalled that symptom as being common to those with concussive head injuries, he didn't know if it was a good or a bad sign of the patient's prognosis. "We'd better get you to a doctor," he announced.

"We'll see about that, " Jenkins replied.

* * *

*Sunday, August 23, 1863. West of the Beaverhead River, high along the trail between Alder Gulch and Bannack.*

Long hours in the saddle had passed without a word being spoken. That was the way things were among those who were comfortable with themselves, each other, and their surroundings. Fine weather and fine scenery added to the calming effects of slow travel on horseback. Since they couldn't much shorten the hours needed to reach Bannack, they were not in any hurry to wear out their mounts.

Rob's mind repeatedly filled with cherished moments from his early days together with Bridget: their small wedding in Dundee, Illinois; their daughter Catherine's birth; their first home in Darien, Wisconsin; their first milk cow. The catalogue of his family memories went on and on. He didn't often let his mind wander through those parts that contained heavy doses of Bridget. Missing her as he did, a danger existed of his lapsing into a depressive state–something he could not afford. That knowledge kept him vigilant not to overspend time in the pages of those recollections.

Lonnie had memories of his own to consider as the miles passed. He had never told Rob of the amazing similarities between Rob's horse, Bricks, and Lonnie's first horse, Brutus. Size, color, conformation, head shape and demeanor were all identical, as if the two were twins. It did not seem possible that the two horses were brothers; Bricks was nearly twenty-five years younger than Brutus would be, had he still been alive. Even the small white-colored coronet above the left rear hoof was there, just as it was on Brutus and his sire. Brutus had no offspring, of that Lonnie was certain. Could Lonnie's father have bred his big favorite stallion, Orpheus, one last time? There was no way to ever know for sure. Yet, what where the chances?

Victor was his usual calm, placid self. A keen-eyed observer might notice that the man was fully alert, aware of all his surroundings, yet seeming to nap in the saddle. No one save Victor knew what he was thinking, what visions he contemplated past and future. He had cultivated the ability to rest and think as he rode along on horseback, whether alone or in the company of others. His spirit informed him that something had gone amiss with the wagonload of gold. Victor knew with certainty that Oce-asay was unhurt; he was equally certain that at least one life would be lost as a result of this gold trove that was behind them. Without giving an explanation of what inspired his counsel, Victor broke the silence by saying, "We should move faster now. Wilson, Oce-asay need us." He was absolutely correct.

Having picked up the pace of their travel in response to Victor's prompting, Rob, Lonnie and Victor soon descended into the Grasshopper Creek valley. They had almost reached the town of Bannack when the rider caught up to them. Even as accustomed as he and his horses were to fast-paced rides over long distances, both Wilson and his mount were winded as he rode up behind his three friends. Wilson wisely slowed his horse to a trot and then a walk, circling the threesome as both he and his horse took in huge gasps of air.

Finally, when Wilson had caught enough breath to speak, he gasped out the words, "We got trouble now (pause) Emry has Doyle at gunpoint (pause) Taking wagon outh (pause) Babcock and others following." He continued to gulp air, but jumped nimbly from the saddle, allowing his horse to better breathe while being led in slow circles around the mounted threesome.

Waiting until Wilson's breathing was more normal, Finn asked, "Is anyone hurt, John?"

Wilson took the time to explain that Doyle had been hit on the head with a rock but appeared to be fine. When Wilson left to bring the news to Finn and company, there had been no other injuries. Emry was making all sorts of demands and threatening to shoot Doyle if anyone tried to come near or rush him. He and Doyle were driving the wagon south, planning to take a much -ess traveled route to get to Denver, Emry's stated destination. "Babcock said to tell you that they would follow Emry all the way there, if necessary, and that Oce-asay was safe with them," were Wilson's closing words of his tale.

When they arrived in Bannack, the foursome hitched their horses after dismounting in front of Goodrich's Hotel. After telling Wilson to look after his horse and take care of himself, Finn set off with Lonnie and Victor to visit George Crisman in his store. George was there, but was elbow-deep dealing with demanding customers. He saw Rob enter with his two companions and signaled that it would take him a few minutes to free himself for a parley. Rob signified that the delay was acceptable, that he would be back shortly. He asked Victor and Lonnie to wait for him back at the hotel.

Rob was off to find Plummer, who kept a small office in the rear of Crisman's building. Since it had its own outside entrance, he figured it would be easier to go outside and around back than to try to wade through the customers in the store.

He found Henry seated at a small table, cleaning his revolvers meticulously and with a great deal of energy. His agitation would be evident to anyone watching.

"Good afternoon t' ya, Henry," behind his natural smile, Rob put as much cheer into his words as he dared. "How're the newly wedded Mr. an' Mrs. Plummer getting along these days?" His greeting was intended as a polite way of opening the conversation, perhaps even calm the sheriff from whatever was troubling him. What news Rob had to share would surely add to whatever was on the man's mind.

Plummer had always been straightforward with Finn, and today's reply was no different. "We're as out of sorts as two people can be, is how we are, Rob." Plummer paused while placing a loaded revolver carefully on the table before him. The force of self-control the man employed was noticeable to Finn's watchful gaze. Plummer then added, "But thanks for asking." He made no attempt to hide the sarcasm he felt.

Plummer listened quietly as Rob explained the situation with Emry, including the evidence of his involvement in the robberies and the murder of Daniels. When Rob told Henry how his name had been used with the Sioux Indians who had carried out Emry's orders, Plummer's face went pale. "That explains some things," he commented. He did continue the conversation, but on an entirely different tack.

"I've got a man in the jail this week, a Peter Horen. I don't suppose you know him?" Plummer looked up to meet Finn's eyes, waiting for an answer. Rob shook his head.

"No, Ah don't, Henry. Would it matter?"

"Not unless you could vouch for his claim that he had no idea his partner was robbing him blind." Plummer was back to finishing his work with the second pistol. Though his right hand and arm would never be as fast or nimble as they had once been, detailed exercises, such as working with the pistol, improved his dexterity. He looked up again to say, "Seems Peter shot his partner during a quarrel. The partner, Lawrence John Keeley, died.

Burchette wants to try him for murder. Says he's sure it was all premeditated." A storm cloud of anger took possession of Plummer's face. "How in the world could our elected judge know that?" He placed the cleaned revolver heavily on the table next to its mate, ready to be loaded. "The trial's set for Monday. If it goes as I expect, I'll be building a gallows to hang Mr. Horen from, though I'm not sure there'll be any justice in it." He was clearly disgusted by this thought.

"It's a sad an' sorry thing if it comes to that, Henry, and I don't envy yer job in carryin' out the execution. Ah'm a little concerned that your name is rumored t' be mixed up in some of the gold shipment robberies, but at least now there's plain evidence that Emry is behind both the robberies an' the spreading of your name." Finn wanted Plummer to know he would support him in clearing any suspicions others had regarding this subject.

"Rob, you've been a good friend and I do thank you for what you're trying to do. But don't worry about me. I'm sending Electa back to her family in Iowa, and I'll be following her in a few short months. It's more her decision than mine. After all the delay in finally getting married, she's decided that the life of a mining town sheriff's wife is not for her. She doesn't like the hours I work, nor that I'm gone from home so much. So it's been decided. She'll be taking the stage to Salt Lake City, then on to Cedar Rapids in Iowa from there. I'll be busy here until after the trial, but then I'm going to ride along with the stage as far as Salt

Lake City to see her off. I'll join her in Iowa by the end of the year; sooner if I can."

There was a certainty, a finality, and a sadness to Plummer's words. Rob had never seen this in the man before today. Finn could offer no words of comfort or advice. Under the circumstances, all he could do was to make an offer of help, then state his own plan of action.

"If there's anything Ah can do to help, I hope y'll let me know. For right now, I need t' make some arrangements for another wagon an' get after Emry and the gold he's made off with. Meanwhile, Lonnie and I are off to fetch Emry's hoard. I'm going to tell ya exactly where it's hidden. When we dig it up, we're goin' t' leave five pounds of gold there, just in case. Not a fortune, but enough t' help ya out if ya need it. It ya don't, just leave it there. It's well enough where it is." Rob proceeded to give Plummer specific directions to find the stash, which was no more than ten or eleven miles from where they stood.

He had no sooner finished his verbal map than George Crisman came in. "Sorry I took so long, Rob. Saturday customers can be pretty demanding, and I've not been in the store but three days this week. How've you been and what can I help you with?" He paused before adding, "Oh and here's two telegrams the stage brought in for you while you were away."

Rob took the envelopes, as the two of them walked away from the door to Plummer's office, then explained that he would need to keep Crisman's wagon and horse team a good deal longer, without explaining the details. And since he had reason to believe the rig might never return to Bannack, he offered to pay a premium price to buy it outright. Crisman thought about it, then decided he could afford a new setup for the sum Rob offered. He accepted the deal on the spot, insisting upon gold for payment. George was fair and kindly, but no fool. This was Bannack, after all.

Finn thanked him for his understanding and promised to produce the payment presently. He added that he desperately needed yet another wagon and team, and pressed George to suggest anyone having them available, even if they weren't looking to sell just now.

Crisman willingly provided the name of a local teamster together with where and when Rob might best contact the man. They had concluded that business talk when Crisman changed the subject completely. "What's eatin' at Henry, Rob? He hasn't been himself the last few days when I've seen him. Is his new bride gnawing at him already?" Though he smiled, Crisman was concerned. Henry Plummer was a friend and George wanted to help if he could.

"It's not what ya might think of in that way, George. Henry's got a lot on his mind with the coming trial. As for his wife ... well, he is sending her t' relatives in Iowa for awhile ... at least 'til things become more settled-down out here in the mining districts." Rob didn't feel it his place to reveal more details. The whole town and district would learn of Electa's leaving soon enough, so he felt it acceptable to share that fact.

Finn told Crisman to expect payment for the wagon rig before the end of the day. Crisman's reply was in the form of assuring Rob of his confidence that he was "good for it", and the two men parted just outside the Crisman store. As Finn headed to the Goodrich Hotel, Plummer caught up with him matching his stride.

Henry must have overheard Finn talking to Crisman. "Thanks for not sayin' any more than you did, Rob. Crisman's a good man and a friend, but I need to keep my plans for leaving the territory private for now. Seems there's a some trouble brewin', and I aim to put any involving my name to rest before I leave and before anyone gets wind of my plans. So I'll thank you again for keeping things that way." Plummer's voice was calmer, flatter than it had been. There was no evidence of the agitation that Finn had noticed earlier.

"As for that other matter, the hidden stash you told me about," Plummer paused while carefully choosing his words, "I can't thank you enough for the offer, though I cannot imagine that I'll ever take you up on it. Go ahead and clean out the trove completely, Rob. No sense leaving it untouched forever after all the work and trouble that's gone into getting it."

Rob wasn't surprised at hearing Plummer's thoughts. He believed the man to be good and on the right path of restoring his own standing and reputation. Perhaps a little more time doing his job as sheriff would take care of both those issues and he could leave with a clean slate. Especially if the man didn't have the distraction of caring for a new bride. Rob hoped so. "We'll see, Henry. Maybe we'll leave ya a portion for a rainy day..."

"Take it all, Rob! Really!" Plummer interrupted. Though he kept his voice low, the emphasis grew noticeably. "I don't need the gold! And I don't need the temptation!" His earlier stress was beginning to return to his features as he pushed his words through gritted teeth.

"As ya wish then, Henry. Ah've no desire t' add t' yer troubles. But please, call on me if Ah can be of any help. Ah think you know that Ah trust ya an' consider ya a friend." Rob's words carried considerable emphasis.

The two friends parted in the middle of Bannack's main street; Plummer returning to his office, Finn searching for Conover, the stage and freight company man recommended by Crisman. As they parted, Finn noticed that Plummer had his brace of pistols holstered and ready for whatever trouble lay ahead. Since his right hand was mostly useless for gunplay now, the revolver on that side was in the reverse-draw position–it would serve only as a back up to its mate in the left holster. Plummer no longer had the option of drawing two guns at once.

Once inside the hotel, Rob immediately inquired of Conover's whereabouts. Bill Goodrich jerked a thumb over his shoulder and replied, "If yer quick enough, ya just might catch him leaving town out the back way. Takin' the wagon trail over to Virginia City." Rob nodded his head in thanks and wasted no time following the direction Goodrich had indicated.

Good fortune was with him again, as Conover heard Rob's shouts and halted his progress, then was agreeable to part with a wagon for the right price. They hung up briefly over a team to draw the freighter. Rob could not settle for the pair of oxen being offered—oxen would be too slow to catch up with his unspoken quarry. Conover would not hear of parting with even a single horse; they were essential to his stage business. They finally agreed upon a team of aging mules, though Rob felt he'd been bested on the price for them. After all, he was in urgent need and it showed in his demeanor. Finally, the two men shook on the deal and Rob went back to the hotel to find Lonnie.

Walters had looked after Roxie and Bricks, making sure they were watered, groomed and fed. Victor and Wilson had insisted on caring for their own mounts. The horses were saddled and hitched before a trough at the stable. Wilson had told Walters that, so long as there was no hard riding required for the next twenty-four hours, both his horse and he could resume the trail with the other three.

Rob sent Lonnie back to the stable to inform Victor and Wilson of time and place for his planned meeting. Finn would share final details with thembefore leaving Bannack this evening. He himself went back to settle his accounts with Crisman and Conover. Since he kept his gold supply in Crisman's safe, these details were relatively quick and easy.

When the foursome met together again the same evening, it was in the Goodrich Hotel dining room. They sat down to their meal with plenty of enthusiasm for the food and for the companionship. They'd spent many days together dealing with the Ogden gold trove, more days figuring out the questions surrounding Emry, Daniels, and the Sioux indians. Gold had been at the center of all their attention these past weeks, yet none of them were possessed by the "gold-fever" commonplace in mining towns. Rob laid out the next steps of his plan while they ate. All were careful to keep their voices low to prevent listening ears picking up their conversation. As usual, they were at a table tucked into the back corner of the room.

After their meal, Rob adjourned first to retrieve the mule-drawn freight wagon from the Oliver-Conover livery barn. He had no trouble maneuvering it back to the hotel, where the others waited with their assorted baggage and paraphernalia, his own and Lonnie's making up the bulk of it. Both Victor and Wilson always traveled very light. Lonnie had already settled all their fees with Goodrich–it was unlikely they would be returning to Bannack any time soon, if ever.

When they finally left town, Bricks was on a tether behind the wagon, as was Wilson's mount–Wilson and Rob rode on the freighter's high bench seat. Everyone's extra gear was in the bed of the big wagon. Included therein were a pick and two shovels. Walters and Victor rode their mounts along on each side of the wagon. Darkness fell as the caravan thus composed drove eastward from Bannack to retrieve the robbers' stash of gold. The waxing moon, when it rose, would give them plenty of light to work by.

Whether they and the mules would have enough light to travel by was another matter. Grasshopper Creek's gulch was narrow and winding; in many places requiring some creative wagon handling to negotiate in daylight. Darkness made it all the more challenging, and having an unfamiliar rig and an unknown mule team added to the difficulty facing this portion of the trip. But they had all agreed at dinner that their best chance for success would be to secretly recover the stolen gold, and darkness provided the only avenue for such secrecy. That and the fact they were not on the usual wagon route.

Clattering their way along the undeveloped track took much longer in the darkness than expected. Finally, the half moon broke through the clouds hanging above and they were able to increase their forward progress. Even so, it was after midnight before they reached their destination. Victor had keen hearing and night vision; Finn asked him to take a watchful position above them while the other three went to dig out the hidden treasure cache.

As the last pouches of gold were being loaded into the sturdy freight wagon, Victor was suddenly at Rob's side. "Five men on foot." Victor pointed, "Two there ... two there ... one there," indicating two locations bracketing their own, plus one on the trail behind. Wilson moved to stealthily pick up his Spencer repeating carbine. He handed Rob's Sharps rifle over noiselessly. Lonnie and Victor each held a loaded coach gun at the ready.

Rob motioned for his three companions to get behind covering rocks, while he took a position that put the wagon between him and their pursuers before calling out, "Who goes there? What is your business?" His voice was clear and strong with no trace of his Irish brogue nor the fear he felt.

"Ya don't need to know who we are. Just drop yer guns an' leave the wagon where it stands. Go back the way ya came and don't look back, ya dirty mick!" The owner of the voice could have been any one of a hundred or more men who called Bannack home. By his use of a derogatory epithet toward Rob, they were reasonably certain it was not another Irishman. But that scarcely narrowed the possibilities.

Rob laid down and rolled under the wagon, where he was hidden in deep shadow. A gunshot rang out in the darkness, the bullet striking the wagon side immediately above where Rob now lay. It would have hit him in the upper body were he yet standing where he had been. That shot also betrayed the location of the shooter by its muzzle flash. Wilson's carbine spoke once, then silence fell over the scene.

After a wait of perhaps thirty seconds, a voice called, "Hart? You okay?" to which there was no answer.

Another voice yelled, "Rush 'em, now!"

Moments later the four men at the wagon heard scuffling from several directions and each man turned to face his attackers. Kneeling down and hunched against the rocky walls of the ravine and from under the wagon, they had the advantage of superior cover and backlighting against the aggressors. Each of the shotguns fired once followed by Rob's Colt pistol and Wilson's carbine. Grunts and groans coming from their targets told the shooters they had found their marks. The sound of a pair of feet running away to the north side of the creek's canyon revealed one of their attackers trying to escape; perhaps to bring others back.

Rob shouldered the big rifle, sighting toward the far hillside, now bathed in moonlight. He figured there was a chance their adversary would show himself as he moved to escape the narrow valley. Rob's thumb carefully cocked the hammer, then he activated the set-trigger. A light touch on the main trigger would fire the accurate gun. He didn't have long to wait.

The crack of his Sharps came as a surprise to Rob's three companions, as well as to the one surviving attacker lying nearby, and to the man across the valley, Rob's target, who had nearly escaped. Unlike assassination shots made in the past, Rob felt no guilt, no remorse. This was no assassination. Whoever the downed man was, he was clearly an enemy bent on an ill purpose. And he had made the first move. Rob's shot was made responsively to save himself and his companions. They would be easy prey if pursued by men on horseback while driving the slow-moving wagon. His focus now was on the hope that there were no reinforcements near enough to have heard the exchange of gunfire.

Moving cautiously in widening circles to discover their downed attackers only took them a few minutes. Three men were dead where they lay. Not one of them was known to Finn, Walters, nor Victor. Though Wilson said he thought he recognized two of the faces, he did not know their names. The fourth man was breathing roughly, his life nearly gone. As the man's lips moved, Rob leaned his ear close and heard the hoarse whisper, "The brothers will have the last word in this." The man's last gasp pushed out his final words.

Rob stood up, carefully reloaded his Sharps and instructed the others, "Check the wagon an' mules, then get back on the trail east. Leave these four where they lay; there's nothing t' be done about them right now. Ah'll cross over the creek an' get up the other side. It shouldn't take me long. If Ah need help, Ah'll fire three shots from the Colt. Lonnie, you drive the wagon, an' don't stop for anything. Victor, please stay with Lonnie. John, Ah'm countin' on you t' back me up if ya hear my three shots. Otherwise just keep on until Ah rejoin ya." All three listeners nodded their understanding in unison.

Rob mounted Bricks, reined him around and rode into the shadows in the direction of the creek and the hillside beyond.  Lonnie checked the wagon before climbing to the seat, taking the traces in hand, and gently encouraging the team forward.  Victor and Wilson mounted their horses, Victor taking the lead with Wilson following along behind the wagon.  All of them, man and beast, were on high alert for sounds or movements in the night.

Once they reached the crest of the hill overlooking the Grasshopper Creek valley behind them, Rob and Bricks halted.  They'd come up slowly as Rob watched the ground they tread upon and the distances ahead for signs of movement, tracks or blood.  All he had seen thus far were a few small spots along the way.  Dismounting at the first of these, he easily confirmed that they were freshly made by a wounded critter.  Since they were exactly in line with where his quarry had been when Rob fired, it was safe to assume the blood trail belonged to that man.

Now that they were at the top of the climb, the land opened out onto a level bench before them, running parallel to the valley below.  The bench was perhaps two hundred yards wide to the north, varying as the roots of the hills came out to meet the rim of the gulch.  Brush and shadows challenged even Rob's acute eyesight by playing tricks with the intermittent moonlight.  Everything seemed to be a man hiding behind a bush.  The next moment, stationary objects appeared to move.

Rob had no choice but to dismount and track on foot. The Sharps would be cumbersome for this stalk; he considered leaving the big gun in the scabbard. It could be that the man he was following was only slightly wounded and still able to scramble ahead. Most likely any shooting would be done at close range with his pistol, but he had best prepare for any eventuality.

Good as Bricks was as mount and friend, the big gelding was not quiet in a setting such as this. Rob tied him to a stout bush and eased the Sharps rifle from its scabbard. Before leaving Bricks' side, he checked to ensure the horse was in no danger of falling back down the way they had just come up.

Finn checked ahead before placing each foot, lest he give away his own position by snapping a twig or misstepping on a rock. He was in a partial crouch to reduce his tall silhouette against the night sky.

Minutes passed slowly with little distance covered. Rob felt the bullet's impact in the split second before he heard the shot. Pain coursed through his arm and shoulder from the wound to his upper left arm. Aware at once that the shot had come from behind, he spun around, drawing his Colt revolver in the process, then dropped to his knee. Bricks' loud snort was followed closely by the cracking sound of a horse's hoof connecting with human flesh and bone followed by the sound of a body tumbling into the valley below.

Silence returned for the moment, but when he heard the sound of Bricks pawing the ground, Rob hurriedly retraced his steps to where the horse remained tied. The bullet wound in his arm, while not superficial, did not need immediate tending to. His examination of Bricks revealed no injuries to the horse, for which he was greatly relieved. Still clutching the Sharps in a position of readiness, he walked in a widening pattern of circles to discover what had taken place.

He found evidence indicating the assailant had crept along the edge of the drop-off while Finn rode up after him, then hunkered down to await the arrival of his lone pursuer. It occurred to Rob that the best shot his adversary had would have been before he dismounted. Why had the man waited? He would probably never learn the answer. He visually surveyed the entire bench area as best he could from where he stood next to Bricks, listening carefully for sounds of any other human activity. After another several minutes' wait, during which the night continued absolutely silent, he turned, untied his horse and led him carefully down the embankment.

No human neck could make such an angle unless it was broken. It didn't take a doctor to make that diagnosis. But upon closer inspection, Rob decided that the hoof which smashed in the man's face was more likely what killed him. He'd probably been dead before landing on the valley floor. This was the second time one of Bricks' hooves had saved Finn on a mission in darkness. Rob's affection for his four-legged friend again grew.

He had no idea of the man's identity and didn't care. What was needful now was to rejoin his companions and take up the hunt for Emry, wherever he was leading the BMI men and Oce-asay. Everything else would have to sort itself out in due time.

The cool, rushing waters of Grasshopper Creek were again at hand, so, while Bricks occasionally drank, Rob tended his latest injury. He removed his coat and shirt, then soaked his bandana in the cold water and used it to thoroughly wash the holes in his arm. The projectile had passed through cleanly. "Lucky it didn't hit the bone," he said to himself as he worked on the arm. Because the water was so cold, it helped numb his flesh. There wasn't much pain when he wrapped the rung-out cloth around the wound and tied it.

Once he was again dressed, he spoke gently to Bricks, and hugged the big animal around the neck affectionately. Rob was truly thankful for his loyal equine friend. He climbed into the saddle and made sure they were headed downstream before letting the reins go slack to allow Bricks to choose his own course and pace. They had only ridden a few hundred yards before spotting a rider ahead of them, coming their way.

"Rob! Are ya alright?" John Wilson called out.

Finn's relief overcame his upset that his orders had not been followed. "Ah'm fine John, but Ah thought ya understood not ..."

"We took a vote and your orders lost, Rob. We decided you were more important than the gold. Victor and Lonnie are less than a half-mile from here. That's all the further we got when we heard the gunshot."

Though Wilson's face was hidden in the dark, Rob easily imagined the wide grin probably plastered there. Finn knew he was fortunate that things this night turned out as well as they had.

\* \* \*

*Monday, August 24, 1863. At the confluence of Grasshopper Creek and the Beaverhead River, Idaho Territory.*

By the time they reached the mouth where Grasshopper Creek joined the Beaverhead River, the sun was well up. Having an unobstructed view in all directions was an important consideration after the developments of the previous night. They decided to make a hasty camp and share a meal. Victor and Lonnie both took the opportunity to examine and treat Rob's bullet wound.

Before getting deeply into a discussion of what they were facing and what route their travel might take, Wilson encouraged Rob to recount the events that took place the night before, when he tracked their last attacker. He told the story in detail. Wilson hung on every detail of Rob's story and description of the dead man he'd found on the floor of the valley. After explaining how Bricks had dispatched the man who had shot Rob, there was enthusiastic approval for the horse's action all around. Wilson commented to Finn, "You sure had the luck of the Irish last night."

Praise for Bricks' obvious intelligence was glowing; none could recall a horse of such abilities. All except Lonnie, who was privately remembering that his horse Brutus from childhood years, and Brutus' sire were the smartest equines he had encountered in his life. This trait made Lonnie even more certain that Bricks was the product of his father's horse-breeding efforts.

Victor showed no concern about finding Oce-asay, knowing the young warrior could handle himself in any circumstances. Lonnie pronounced Rob's wound to be fine, all things considered, recommending only the addition of a sling and that Rob should ride on the wagon for a few days. Wilson agreed with the overall plan, which left only the question: Which direction should they first take, northward or southward? They needed to find Emry and then get to Denver as quickly as possible. Wilson had the most recent information impacting that decision.

John told the others, "When I left yesterday to find you, Emry was on the wagon heading south along the Beaverhead. Babcock, Thatcher, and Oce-asay were on horseback; Doyle was driving the team. That would have been maybe thirty miles north of here. Emry said he wanted to stay clear of the Indians and Virginia City. Slow as that team was pulling the wagon, they couldn't be more than a couple of miles from us. I can scout upstream for five or six miles, then do the same downstream while you fellas rest." He seemed eager to find their quarry.

"An' that would be much appreciated, John. But it won't be necessary. Ah believe that's Emry an' the others in the distance. Seems our timing couldn't have been any better. Maybe our luck is improving, after all." Rob smiled wryly. They'd need luck and a good plan to thwart Emry's escape without anyone else getting hurt, and Finn was fresh out of good plans.

* * *

*Monday, August 24, 1863. The westbound road outside Lawrence, Kansas.*

Having done what they could to bind wounds and burns, and provide comfort for victims of the raid at Lawrence, it was time for the crew of the Heinz Brothers freighter to again take to the road west. The telegraph wires were now repaired, so Jenkins' message to his employer would be received and word sent ahead notifying customers of the delay. Businesses in Denver would be awaiting the shipment of goods they had ordered from St.

Louis merchants or those further east. With his delivery schedule ever on his mind, Jenks' anxiety was shown in his cranky words and behavior, despite the fact he was not really upset with his two charges. Quite the contrary, he could hardly believe how well the two young men had behaved in the situation they were leaving behind.

The people of Lawrence who had been helped by Patrick, Billy, and Jenkins were grateful and said so. In particular they were impressed by the willingness and experience young Murphy showed, assisted by his one-armed friend, Billy. Several of them spoke together and composed a brief letter to the Kansas governor, extolling the virtues of all three men, but especially Patrick Murphy. His tireless, unceasing efforts bordered on the heroic, they said, and suggested the young man be recognized for his humanitarian spirit. In their letter, they explained that Murphy was a Confederate parolee, the circumstances of his capture, his orderly service in the Union field hospital, and that he was attempting to get west of the States in order to honor his parole.

Eager to make up for lost time, Jenkins pushed his mule team to greater speed than they had yet produced on the road. After all, they had just had a two-and-a-half day rest following right after several slow, easy days. Their new pace would carry them as many as thirty-five miles per day while they pushed longer hours on level ground. That was fast for a freight wagon, but their load was lightened by the robbery and the supplies they gave out to those in need in Lawrence.

* * *

*Wednesday, August 26, 1863. Bannack, Idaho Territory, late afternoon.*

Henry Plummer clapped the dust off his gloved hands. The act was more symbolic than necessary. Hanging a man as part of his sheriff's duties did not put much dirt on his hands. But considering the nature of the trial, its outcome, and the resultant verdict requiring Plummer to end another man's life, he felt about as dirty as he could remember ever being.

He had expressed his opinion to the judge, one B. B. Burchette, who, having been as duly elected by the miners of the district as Plummer had been himself, seemed to swell into the power of his position–that of holding life-or-death decisions over others. This instance was one in which Plummer felt strongly that no such justice should be applied. Two men had quarreled, it got heated, and one shot the other. There were no witnesses and no one testified that any grudge existed between the two partners, which should have ruled out pre-meditation. The killing was a manslaughter, yes. But murder? Hardly. Yet the judge didn't see it that way, and he was the judge, after all.

Plummer finally reconciled himself to the outcome, and his role in it. He did as his elected role required him to do: he oversaw building the gallows and the hanging of the prisoner, Peter Horen. As he walked back to his house he was mumbling to himself, shaking his head from side to side. Neither of these behaviors were common for this man who had self-assuredly killed men before when the circumstances called for it. His contempt for frontier justice had just climbed to a new level and he could not see himself being a part of this system for much longer. His bride's insistence that he quit his elected post and accompany her back to the States was beginning to take on a bit of shine.

Plummer's wife, Electa, was aware of her husband's feelings and, indeed, took some comfort from them. She would be leaving the next week, heading to her aunt's farm in Iowa, a rural area for certain, but one with a great deal more government than would be found in Bannack for some time to come. Henry would ride along for the first leg of her journey, as far as Salt Lake City, and then would be joining her sometime in the fall or early winter. She loved her new husband; worried greatly about his well-being in this city of scoundrels and every type of criminal element. There were good people here as well, to be sure, but they were exceptions. They could stay and work to settle the wildness of this place. She and Henry would be safely in Iowa long before such reforms would be completed.

When Henry Plummer walked through the door of his house and flopped down into one of the chairs at the table, Electa smiled and welcomed him, saying simply, "You look tired, Henry. Can I take your boots?"

\* \* \*

*Wednesday, August 26, 1863. Late afternoon, fifty miles east of Monida Pass, Idaho Territory.*

Peter Doyle was driving the wagon carrying Michel Ogden's trove of gold, leaving Emry seated on the bench seat next to him, free to wave his pistol about, while shouting orders to those around him. His behavior resembled nothing so much as that of a spoiled brat getting his way with permissive parents. But what could they do?

Doyle was under the barrel of Emry's gun. Emry had already shot the man in the foot to prove his own resolve to do violence (and to lessen Doyle's chance of making an escape).

Babcock had conferred with Rob privately about the Treasury Department operative's behavior, explaining that it was becoming noticeably more erratic these past two days. Thinking that it might lead Emry to admit the hopelessness of his situation, Babcock had revealed to Emry, at yelling distance, the truth that it was the Treasury Department that ordered the BMI men to be sent to Bannack. Emry's telegram East had given rise to suspicions there, which led to Babcock and his men being sent on Emry's trail. The revelation had the opposite effect: Emry had become more distracted and detached from the reality of his surroundings, at times talking to Daniels (who was dead) or the Sioux Indians (who were no longer present). He even called out to Wilson as though they were old friends. All the comments Emry was making were incoherent. It was clear the man was becoming more deranged and desperate with each passing hour.

It is difficult enough to predict what a sane person might do in difficult circumstances; with a madman it is impossible. Both Finn and Babcock had taken turns shouting across the distance between the two wagons, attempting to calm Emry and offer peaceful solutions from the current dilemma. In addition to his other symptoms of mental distress, the man was paranoid. He accepted nothing he was told as truth, and verbally lashed out with each offer they made him.

Holding the cocked revolver against Doyle's head, Emry shouted, "That's enough from you, Finn! I've never trusted you or any of you damned Pinkertons. You think you've been clever? You're so clever you found me out, is that it? You're just fools, government pawns, you and your friend Babcock! Just like Daniels! Your government has no interest in saving its people. This gold is not for who you think it is! That's how clever you are!" Emry was shaking like a leaf in the wind. He moved jerkily, he was twitchy. Also, he was no gunman, and his finger was on the trigger that could kill his captive instantly with even a slight touch, accidental or otherwise.

The moment was upon them that Finn and Babcock had earlier discussed and planned for. It was clear there would be no improvement, no reasoning with Emry. Making brief eye contact and with a nod of his head, Rob knelt behind the big freight wagon to mask his actions. Emry was instantly alert, suspicious.

"What! What'ya doin' there, Finn? Show yourself this instant or I'll blow his brains out! I swear I'll do it!"

"Hang on there a minute, Emry," Babcock's voice was firm. "Finn's bandage has come loose–he's bleeding." Babcock's hands were in the air as he took two steps in the opposite direction of where Finn had gone down.

The diversion had the desired effect. Emry waved the pistol at Babcock and yelled, "Get back before I shoot YOU, Babcock!"

While Babcock stepped away, Finn rolled on the ground to get a clear shooting angle. The big bullet from the Sharps rifle entered Emry's head just below his right ear. He was dead and down instantly, dropping the gun and collapsing in a heap where he had been at the wagon seat, the left side of his head gone. Doyle nearly collapsed as well, such was the emotion of the moment. Other than the foot injury Emry had caused him earlier, though, Doyle was unhurt.

# CHAPTER SEVEN

# Families, Friends, and Fates

*Mid-September, 1863. Denver City, Colorado Territory*

During the weeks of the long trek leading up to the South Pass shortcut to Denver, the slow-moving party made up of two Pinkerton detectives, a former U.S. Army cavalryman, and three Bureau of Military Information operatives had passed through vistas more beautiful than any they had seen to date. Birds and game animals of every size and description filled the forests and meadow lands. Twice they made wide detours so as not to disturb families of bears foraging. Water in the streams and rivers was as clear and sweet as any they'd tasted. High mountain escarpments were nearly commonplace and strange phenomena such as steaming or smoking grounds and colorful springs drew their attention as they passed by. Wilson had seen some of these during his years with the Army, but he admitted that they still took his breath away at times.

As often happens on trips such as this, the long hours and days together provide ample and natural opportunity for those traveling together to become better known to one another. This trip was no exception. In fact, the nature of their cargo, being made up of gold and a corpse, probably did much to further the prompting of personal information; nobody really wanted to talk about what and who was in the wagons. Those details would be handled when they safely reached Denver.

So it was that Babcock shared his love of drawing in general and making maps in particular. He begged the others' indulgence to leave him behind on occasion while he finished his notes, charts, graphs, and drawings, always catching up before darkness fell. They didn't mind being one short while Babcock attended his efforts. There had been no one following them, and the only Indians they saw were at great distances being obviously intent upon their own purposes of hunting buffalo.

Peter Doyle talked about his love of the outdoors and fishing for trout. He hoped to one day have a family, but was far from certain whether he would prefer a country life of farming or a city life.

John Wilson chimed his agreement with Doyle's love of the outdoors and admitted his private hope that he would be able to spend most of his days ranching, "right up to my last one–whenever that might be. I just need enough to get my stake for my first acreage. I'm not much for cities," he added.

Lonnie spoke about his love of horses and growing up on his father's horse farm in Kentucky. He considered mentioning his suspicion that Bricks had come from the same farm as he, but decided against doing so for the time being. A personal dream of his that he did share was to one day settle down on a farm where he could breed and train horses, and perhaps be re-united with his sister Radlyn.

Rob told of growing up in Ireland, his love of family and the music of his homeland. He shared the difficult decision of turning his back on his father's law practice, and of crossing the ocean–leaving his family behind. His chest swelled and he waxed joyful when telling of meeting and marrying Bridget, and becoming a father and a farmer. His enthusiasm was less obvious when he spoke of his new bride and their anticipated child. He'd not been in contact with Maggie for so long that his guilt about that fact caused his reluctance to say more.

That left the mystery man, Asa Thatcher, to tell his story. Asa hadn't said much at any time; quiet was his normal mode. He was nearly the same size as Rob, younger by about a dozen years. It took longer for the others to learn about Thatcher due to his private manner. They did eventually find out that he had grown up in Muscatine, Iowa. His family had settled there when it was a tiny backwater river town, dwarfed by the size and traffic of its upstream neighbor, Davenport.

Asa's father raised melons in the rich fertile soil of their small farm near the mighty Mississippi. Asa had been intrigued watching the riverboats and, eventually, steamboat traffic he had seen in the distance from the farm. He imagined becoming an engineer working with steam engines, and had actually worked for a steamboat operator for two years before joining the Union Army. It was his plan to return to Muscatine after the war to pursue his passion for steam engineering.

Of this company, Rob Finn found himself contemplating the man Thatcher more so than the others, even more than Lonnie. Their first meeting had been less than ideal for people soon to be bound together on a mission involving danger and violence. The same fact applied to Peter Doyle. These two operatives were those that had stepped from cover with Babcock to hold Rob, Victor, and Tanahee at gunpoint at their campsite more than a month ago.

In that time, Rob had not once had occasion to question Thatcher's behavior. If anything, he found the unassuming man's presence to be reassuring. It was as though he sensed a kindred spirit present, backing him up, so to speak. He had been present at the confrontation with the Sioux Indians as well as setting the bait and closing the trap for Emry. He stayed with Babcock to guard Emry until Finn, Victor, and Walters could return. Thatcher had intelligent eyes that took in everything while betraying nothing. He showed enough discernment to reserve sharing comment or judgement unless asked. Finn figured the man would be a good ally in a scrape.

\* \* \*

With so many details needing attention, their days in Denver City passed in a flash. All six of the men met with United States Marshal A. C. Hunt to report and give testimony regarding the nature and circumstances of Emry's death. Hunt explained that, since Colorado Territory was yet in the process of formation, he'd record everything and turn it over to whomever had jurisdiction in the matter. Finn's and Walters' Pinkerton badges and the three BMI operatives were confirmed by telegram. It didn't seem there would be any difficulty in putting the matter to rest, but it might take a couple of days. Hunt thanked them, asked where they were staying, and that they not leave Denver before checking with him.

Both Finn and Babcock had superiors expecting reports from their operatives in the field. They drafted brief telegrams and lengthier reports working together to make certain of including all the details of each event. Walters, Wilson, Doyle, and Thatcher often sat in during these sessions to contribute their recollections and insights.

The resultant two documents, each being nearly identical to the other and nearing fifteen pages in length, left out nothing. Nothing except any mention of Michel Ogden's trove, which they unanimously and enthusiastically agreed was none of the government's official business. Such was their commitment to that ideal, they made a pact to never reveal the existence of Ogden's gold outside their group. That treasure was in the trust and safekeeping of Finn, Walters, and Wilson in perpetuity, according to the wishes of those who had given it into their hands. The three of them agreed it would be held in safekeeping on Rob's farm in Delavan.

When they next heard from the U.S. Marshal, it was almost ten days later via a messenger requesting that they meet in Hunt's office. Upon their arrival, they were introduced to the Honorable Moses Hallett, recently of the Territorial Congress, and who was also a local attorney, soon to be appointed district judge by President Lincoln. In addition to his friendship with his fellow Illinoisan occupying the White House, Hallett was well acquainted with Allan Pinkerton. He asked a few questions as follow-up to what the men had already reported to Marshal Hunt, and then pronounced that, as far as he was concerned, the matter was "at rest". In the days between their previous meeting, Hunt had arranged for the burial of Emry's remains. That already having been accomplished, Emry's death, and the manner of it, was completely resolved so far as the law was concerned.

The recovered gold which had been stolen by Timothy Emry was another matter. By direction of the US Treasury Department, the gold recovered from Emry's ill-gotten stash, minus reasonable reduction for expenses, had been put into the care of John Babcock and his remaining BMI deputy operative, Asa Thatcher. Peter Doyle was on leave from his position with the BMI pending his recovery from the gunshot wound Emry had inflicted upon him.

The Treasury Department also required that the precious metal all be coined by the Clark, Gruber and Company Bank and Mint. Finn and Walters arranged for the minting to be done. Babcock and Thatcher joined in overseeing the transfer of the raw material and minting of the new coins. Rob renewed his acquaintances with the Clark brothers of that firm.

This plan also met with favor from Judge Hallett, who let his Masonic connections with the Clark brothers be known. When the minting was completed, the small, stout coin crates were loaded into the heavy freight wagon Rob had purchased from Conover in Bannack, and placed under a military guard. The aging team of two mules were retired and replaced by a team of four younger animals, (again mules), able to easily draw the load.

Once the newly-minted coins of stolen Bannack gold reached St. Louis, the stated intention of the Treasury Department was to open case files for those alleging to have lost their gold to robberies in and around the Bannack mining district. The Department would investigate written and attested claims as they were received.

The plan held no provision to notify anyone in the mining district of the gold being recovered by the Federal government. Nor was provision made for adjudicating the claims. Finally, not even a location nor method of reliably storing and accounting for the coinage was mentioned. Both Babcock and Finn recognized that this could end up being another thin veneer covering corrupt and illegal

operations within the Federal Government. The prospect
of being part of such a scheme, whether complicit or not,
left them uncomfortable. Both men were trying to think of
better ways to return the gold to its rightful owners.

At the close of one such private conversation
between the two men, Babcock turned to Finn and asked
with a smirk, "What's that saying, Rob? Possession is nine-
tenths of the law?"

"So I've heard, John," Rob answered, a puzzled look
on his face.

\* \* \*

Knocking about in a young western city was a new
experience for Patrick Murphy and Billy Adams. The two
had willingly aided Jenks delivering and unloading the
merchandise that had been hauled from St. Louis to
Denver in the freighter. They were high-spirited in their
new circumstances and surroundings, especially since they
were officially free of the war's hold on Patrick.

Jenkins' mood had improved immediately upon
successfully making the last of the deliveries, depositing the
cash and wiring the message and money back to St. Louis.
In fact, he was so happy to be relieved of those burdens, he
let his two young companions talk him into seeing a doctor
about his head injuries. There were still occasions of
blurred vision and headaches, so why not? What could be
the harm?

\* \* \*

*September 17, 1863. Shortly after lunch. Downtown Denver, Colorado Territory.*

The downtown was a much different place to look at since the Great Denver Fire destroyed most of it on April nineteenth. Many buildings had been rebuilt, and many more were under construction. Replacement buildings and repairs were of brick rather than the all-wood construction used earlier, before the fire.

Finn's wound to his left arm had not given him any trouble and Walters admitted it appeared to be healing as it should. Nonetheless, his regular insistence that Rob have their old friend look at it paid off when the stubborn patient finally relented and agreed to go along with Lonnie's urgings.

They found the building, where it had stood before the fire, with a newly rebuilt brick facade and improved roof. Once inside, they found additional new features from what Rob and Lonnie recalled from their visit during the winter. Once again, the good doctor was thorough in his examination of Rob's bullet wound. He commended Lonnie's care, and listened carefully to the latter's explanation of Victor's treatments while he still tended to Finn. As McClelland finished re-bandaging the arm, Walters added a comment about Finn's reluctance to seek medical help. Lonnie also made a fuss over the doctor's cat named Talon.

The visit ended after a sling was affixed, Rob was told to rest the limb, and the fee was paid to the doctor for his service. Finn, Walters and Wilson said goodby to the doctor and left the offices.

Two threesomes of men made room for one another to pass by on the stairs. Narrow as the stairway was, handrails had been installed on both sides to assist patients visiting Dr. William F. McClelland, who was likely the best of the few physicians available in the growing city.

Rob Finn, being the broadest-shouldered of the three men going down the stairs, inadvertently bumped the short stocky man leading two youngsters up.

"Ah'll be beggin' yer pardon, then," Rob said cordially as he doffed his hat to the other, his Irish accent plain for all to hear.

"And ya have it wit' no harm done," returned Jenks with equal politeness, his Welsh origin revealed by his articulation. "Good day to ya, sirs," was an added afterthought.

Finn, Walters, and Wilson reached the bottom of the staircase, opened the door and exited the building onto the boardwalk at street level.

The three men had spent so much time together, and been through so many experiences in the past eight weeks, it was hard to accept that their time for parting had arrived. These past two weeks they'd been in Denver taking care of business such as sending telegrams, dealing with the US Marshall and local judge, writing and sending reports, and arranging to mint, protect, and transport gold coins. Plenty more had passed between them, including the settling of a few financial matters. Wilson was reluctant to accept Rob's generous offer of compensation at first. In the end they reached an agreement that both pronounced to be equitable. Now it was time to say farewell.

"I've no plans to visit the Territories in the foreseeable future, John." Finn paused to consider his next words. "So I can't imagine when I might see ya again at Fort Owen." Rob smiled and added, "Of course, yer welcome at the farm in Delavan any time, an' stay as long as ya like. We'd love t' have you there. We've plenty of room."

"You never know, Rob, you just never know. I've been thinking of settling down, taking a wife and making a real home place for a family out by the Hellgate. It's probably about time I think about other work than being a horse messenger, before I get my scalp lifted. Don't worry. I'll deliver your messages to Plummer and Crisman in Bannack before I give it up." John Wilson had the broadest grin of any man Rob had ever known.

Wilson turned to face Lonnie and say his good-bye to another fellow traveler. As he was about to open his mouth, the door behind them burst open, nearly knocking Wilson and Walters into the street. One of the two young men they had just passed on the stairs stumbled, fell, and then picked himself up. He was unhurt, but the red coloring of his cheeks announced his embarrassment for all to see.

He faced Rob squarely and asked, "Excuse me, but would you be Rob Finn? Uh … er … The name came up in the doctor's office … Ah just had t' find out … are ya my brother-in-law?" His outbursts were comical. The young man was so excited that his words were tangled trying to get out.

Rob laughed gently and said, "Well, Ah don't know, lad, there's plenty of Finns about an' plenty of 'em are called Rob. Who would you be, now?"

"Oh sir, my apologies sir, but Ah'm a Murphy … Patrick Murphy … from Ireland … an' me sister's Bridget! Are ya Bridget's Rob Finn?"

Time seemed to stop for Rob when the young man before him finished his question. A lump formed in his throat, and he felt dazed as his mind tried to deal with the question of whether this could actually be Bridget's younger brother Patrick Murphy. After all, Murphy was the most common surname in Ireland, and Patrick the most common name given to boys born there. How could it be even remotely possible?

Finn was already calming himself with the assurance of such thoughts, knowing that the statistical unlikelihood of his Bridget being sister to the young Murphy in front of him was huge. The butterflies in his stomach had about settled when Patrick came out with his next words.

"Ah've got her letter from Wisconsin, sir. But Ah've not had another from her for more than a year. Do ya know the Finns of Darien, there in Wisconsin, sir?" He was breathless from his haste and excitement in getting it all out.

The lad's face reflected the emotional agony of his need to know. Rob couldn't speak for the lump rising the second time in his throat. His vision blurred momentarily as he threw his big arms impulsively around his newly-met brother-in-law, the action making a mess of the sling Doctor McClelland had finished installing on his left arm and shoulder but a few minutes earlier.

Meanwhile, Walters and Wilson moved off a polite few paces to complete their adieus to one another. Wilson needed to get along while the light was in his favor; he had a long distance to cover before he would be back in Fort Owen. His thoughts of what lay ahead for him added to his desire to vacate Denver. He was fond enough of his two traveling companions, to be sure, but the future prospects for his life called the more loudly.

Done with Lonnie, Wilson again turned toward Rob. Rob noticed him waiting politely, and realizing the import of the man's need to leave, excused himself temporarily from Patrick. "Don't worry, lad. Ah'll be right here an' we'll finish our talk."

He turned to face Wilson again. "So then, John. It truly is good-bye for now," Rob composed himself enough to resume where they had left off prior to Patrick Murphy's clumsy interruption. His mind was distracted with the painful knowledge of the information he would soon be sharing with Patrick. But his unfinished business with Wilson was also important. He focused himself to say, "I hope you won't mind my mentioning again the importance of those two messages being only for the eyes of the recipients, especially the one to Henry?" Not wanting to wound Wilson's professional pride, Rob posed the question gently.

"No offense taken, Rob. If my guess is anywhere close to the mark, Plummer will be only too happy to have it. Who knows how things are going in the mining district these days. I'll see he gets it, or my name's not John Wilson!" He grinned his broadest grin, patted Rob's shoulder, stepped off the boardwalk and unhitched and mounted his waiting horse so smoothly that the whole operation seemed to be one fluid movement. In another moment he was merely a tiny figure seen through the dust raised by their rapid passing as he and his horse left the city behind.

With Wilson gone from sight, Rob turned back to Patrick and Lonnie. Quirks of fate had surprised each of them before, but nothing of this magnitude had ever taken place in Rob's or Patrick's life. They had a great deal to sort through and would need some time for the process.

Lonnie was feeling out of place until Rob suggested the three of them adjourn someplace where they could visit comfortably and privately.

Patrick remembered his two friends in the doctor's office and stated his need to inform them of this latest development. It was Lonnie who suggested they use a room in McClelland's offices. He would use the time to do more catching up with his friend, Talon, while Rob and Patrick got better acquainted. Talon was the nearly full-grown cat that Lonnie and Rob had gifted to the doctor last December.

Doctor McClelland showed less surprise when Finn, Walters, and Murphy reappeared together in his outer office than did Billy and Jenkins. The doctor chuckled, "I wondered if we might see you all back in here once this young man caught up with you. All I said was 'having another reluctant patient on the heels of Rob Finn seemed like more punishment than I deserved for one day', and he was off down the stairs after you like a shot."

Kindly as he was, the medical man showed no impatience during the rounds of introductions and explanations taking place while he waited to complete his work. His face broke out in a smile when Talon meowed and rubbed against Lonnie's leg, and again when loud purring erupted from the growing feline as his ears were scratched. McClelland did finally usher the others into a room separate from his work area so that he could complete his examination of Jenkins.

The doctor's assessment of Jenkins was that he did indeed have a concussion, severe enough that he prescribed complete bed rest for at least a week before attempting to resume his work as a teamster  His return to St. Louis would have to wait that much longer at the minimum.

Medical diagnoses didn't always count for much with the members of this group, but both Patrick and Billy were concerned by the number of times Jenks had seemed to lose track of his surroundings and the frequency of his headaches.  They insisted the man follow the doctor's orders, adding that they would stay with him.  There seemed to be nothing else reasonable and humane to do in these circumstances.

Rob and Lonnie exchanged a brief look, then Rob announced, "We could use a bit more restin' up ourselves, an' it won't hurt the horses none.  We've spent plenty of time in the saddle these last few weeks.  Besides having remaining business t' handle here in Denver, I would like t' get t' know my brother-in-law a little bit, now we've met.  Let's see if the hotel next door can accommodate us all, shall we?"

As soon as the hotel accommodations were settled, Rob excused himself from the others and invited Patrick to meet with him privately in his room.  Once behind the closed door, Finn was able to gently share the news of Bridget's death with his young brother-in-law.  There followed a bout of grieving and sadness, as one would expect.  The flow of tears was periodically stopped while one or the other would share a fond memory of the departed soul whom both had loved so dearly.

Though he seldom drank intoxicants, Rob ordered mugs of beer brought to the room, telling the bellman to check on them "every half-hour or so." Finally, after several hours and several pints, it seemed the initial emotional blast associated with the death of one so loved was passing. When the bellman next appeared, Rob's order for two shots of "the best Irish whiskey in the house" surprised himself almost as much as it did Patrick.

Being that neither of them were regular partakers of alcohol, the whiskey had a great effect. Both men were passed out, sleeping it off. They awoke embarrassed and reserved and ready to move on.

Their closeness and fondness for one another grew quickly in the next days. It seemed to them both, and to their fellow acquaintances that these two were much more like brothers than in-laws.

\* \* \*

*Wednesday, September 23, 1863. Denver, Colorado Territory.*

Some of life's knottiest problems have ways of working out their own solutions. Judge Hallett liked Babcock's suggestion for a small military escort to accompany the gold shipment back to the States. Arranging for the Army to provide mounted troopers for the guard detail would delay their leaving Denver for a few more days, but would be worth the wait in terms of ensuring the shipment would be secure from robbery or attack as it traveled eastward. There were plenty of hostile Indians in the eastern parts of Colorado Territory, as well as outlaw gangs in Kansas and Missouri, making the precaution a wise one. The wagon would be slow-moving due to the weight of its cargo, making the escort even more attractive to those responsible for the safe arrival of the shipment.

Using the additional time provided by the delay, Finn and Walters set about upgrading their wagon and team for the journey. Finding a better wagon in this growing city might be difficult as the demand was high during the rapid growth and rebuilding. The same could be true for finding a better team to draw the wagon. The best place to start would be at the livery stable where they were keeping Bricks and Roxie.

Waggoner's Livery was on Blake Street near their hotel. Their horses had been treated well, the prices were fair, the operator seemed friendly and honest. Barney Ford, as he was called, was also a barber and operated his barber shop during certain hours in a ground floor shop in the hotel. Due to both men being of mixed racial heritage, Lonnie and Barney had a natural affinity for one another.

Ford listened to the specific features Walters list as most important: sturdy bed and axles, high sideboards, large wheels, and rigged for a team of four or more draft animals. It sounded to him like his customers were wanting to purchase a freight wagon that didn't look like a freight wagon. When he remarked to that effect, Lonnie chuckled and agreed, "That's exactly what we want, Barney. And we'll be looking to sell our current rig as well. Can you help us?"

Ford was quick to point out that selling any rig would be easy due to the present high demand in Denver. He paused for a moment, then explained that he had an older rig available that could be modified to their specifications. He knew of a Swedish wheelwright who did exceptional work, could provide whatever improvements were needed, and might be persuaded to meet their timetable for leaving the city. But first he wanted them to see the wagon he had in mind. Ford kept it in a barn on his property two streets north of his businesses on Blake Street.

Before opening the barn door, Barney warned the two Pinkertons that the wagon might not be exactly what they were expecting to see. Then he opened the door, stepped aside and watched his two customers.

Lonnie looked at Rob, who looked back at him. They both looked at the wagon again, then turned and looked at each other again, and burst out laughing. Poor Barney thought their laughter meant they were rejecting his merchandise. He was personally invested in the wagon because it was the one he had used to cross the plains when he had ventured from Chicago to Denver. He was proud of the old wagon.

Noting the look of distress on his host's face, Rob was quick to say, "This may be just exactly what we're needing. What d'ya think, Lonnie?"

Lonnie nodded agreement and said, "Yessir. This could be just about perfect. A little paint, bigger wheels. Does that front truck turn a full half-circle, Barney?"

Ford's face had already brightened. "Near enough, it does. And she don't bind at all, 'cause of the longer axle and these two stops here. See?" He was pointing under the front of the wagon to draw attention to the sturdy construction features of the frame. "This here wagon was built for a circus. They're always built extra strong for all the weight they carry. And that's why she's painted up in white and red the way she is." He stopped to let Walters and Finn take in more of the wagon's appearance.

What was before them was a completely enclosed, roofed structure on wheels. As Ford had pointed out, it was definitely manufactured for circus use. People lived in these houses-on-wheels for months at a time, hauling around all manner of heavy equipment and gear for their acts. They could sleep inside at night with a solid roof over their heads, instead of the canvas of prairie schooner designs. It certainly looked sturdy enough for their intended cargo. They might not even need to replace the wheels for larger sizes; the wheels on the wagon were taller than all but what a big freight wagon would have. And these wheels were noticeably wider than those of a freight wagon.

Finn and Walters were both favorably inclined to the purchase, but wanted to try out the wagon with a good team of draft animals before agreeing to the deal. Barney filled both requirements within the hour by selecting and hitching a team of four mules, naming his asking price, then telling the two men to take the rig for a ride out of town and back. He knew these men and their attachment to their horses in his stable; he knew they'd be back.

Lonnie handled the traces as well as the team handled the wagon. The combination was as near ideal as he could imagine–a considerable endorsement from one who knew horses as well as he did. Ford had greased the axles before they left the yard. There was not so much as a creak or a squeak from a wheel or a spring. That was another nice detail. Circus people were particular about their comforts while living on the roads of the country, so their wagons had springs under the seats and even heavy-duty carriage springs between the wagon bed and frame. These two features would make this wagon a luxury compared to the buck wagons they'd been accustomed to using.

Upon their return to Ford's barn they pulled up and began to unhitch the mules and lead them into the stalls in the barn. Barney showed up before the job was done. Rob and Lonnie had already discussed the purchase during their ride back into town.

Walters was first to speak, "Barney, I think you've got yourself a deal, if you can take our wagon and the two old nags off our hands. It'll help us if you can tell us where we might find some paint and a couple of brushes." He smiled at the proprietor, who was already beaming back at him.

"That I surely can, Mr. Walters! Don't you worry about that! What color paint would you like?"

The three men exchanged a friendly laugh and finished the chores of putting away the animals and the wagon for the night. The price and terms were already agreed upon. Finn and Walters waited while Ford closed the livery office, hanging a sign saying, "Inquire At Hotel Lobby," and the three of them walked to the hotel together.

Before being seated for a celebratory meal, they sent a messenger with a note inviting Babcock and Thatcher to join them. Similary, the desk clerk sent a bellman to invite Jenkins, Patrick, and Billy downstairs to join the party for dinner. Before long, the eight of them were seated around a large table in the dining room. All eight of the diners noticed that the maître-d' and the waitstaff took special care in seeing to their comfort. Only one of the diners knew that Barney L. Ford was the owner of the entire hotel establishment.

Many topics relating to their upcoming journey back to the States were discussed during dinner, though none of a private nature. The detectives wanted Ford to arrange for his recommended wheelwright, Brian Oman, to make a few alterations and look the wagon over entirely, which Ford readily agreed to have done the next day. The new owners planned that any recommendations Oman made would be carried out as soon as possible, together with the slight enhancements they had in mind.

Among the happiest pieces of information shared that evening was one received unexpectedly while they were at the marshal's office earlier in the day. Governor Evans had been contacted by the Governor of Kansas, who granted a full pardon to Patrick Murphy for his humanitarian work done in Lawrence, Kansas. Having a gubernatorial pardon meant Patrick would no longer be bound by the terms of his military parole. Patrick could travel where he pleased.

Arrangements for the military escort of the shipments headed to St. Louis were nearly complete, needing only the assignment of an appropriate officer to be in charge of the detail. One was expected to arrive within the next two or three days, which gave them time to finish work on the new wagon, including the paint job. Patrick and Billy agreed to handle this chore at a fair rate of pay, so they were looking forward to it. Final loading and adjustment of the loads would be done before they set out.

Jenkins seemed fine during the dinner and insisted that he was fit and ready for the return trip to St. Louis. After receiving a telegram of inquiry from Rob Finn in

Denver, Jeff Heinz wired back agreeing to terms for his driver and wagon to carry a shipment of Denver-minted gold coins to St. Louis at the current Treasury Department rate. Heinz believed having a government-provided military escort to be good security. And since it was at no charge to his firm, this detail sweetened the deal for Heinz. Even though his political sentiments did not agree with the Union government, their troopers would protect his driver, wagon, mules and cargo from attacks by outlaws and renegades. His opinions were private and known to few, including Rob Finn.

Jeffrey Heinz also knew that several contingents of Knights of the Golden Circle members were en-route from Virginia to various gold and silver mining areas in the western territories. As a sympathizer of that group, he knew many of their plans. This time, however, he was hoping to avoid their direct involvement due to his friend Rob's request that the shipment "not be in anyway compromised, challenged, or waylaid." And he had honored that request by not sharing details of the shipments with any of his KGC contacts or informants. He trusted Rob, just as Rob trusted him.

\* \* \*

*Friday, September 25, 1863. On a remote trail crossing east-central Nebraska.*

A wry smile flitted across the face of the mounted messenger. Knowing there was no one within hearing distance, he spoke his true feelings aloud. "Of course Plummer would love to know all the details about Emry and the gold that you found, Rob Finn. But it ain't never gonna happen. My biggest mistake with Emry was trustin' him to run things when I couldn't be around. Don't you worry none though, Mister Pink-er-ton Dee-tec-tive. I will be visiting you. That'll be long before you ever get home to Delavan. You'll see me soon enough."

Wilson then did a little wiggle in his saddle, showing his delight that he was finally about to be rich beyond his wildest expectations. He chortled to himself again when he read the message that Finn had written to Crisman encouraging George to "stand by Plummer" through any upcoming "dark days" or "seeming wrong-doings". Finn's message promised that he and Walters could attest to and prove Plummer's innocence as well as Emry's guilt. "What George don't know won't hurt him ... or me," Wilson giggled. He crumpled the two messages before returning them to his saddle bag. He finished his speech with, "Or my name isn't John Wilson," and continued laughing to himself for a while longer, as he rode on.

John continued to ride north-by-northeast after crossing the Missouri River at Omaha and leaving Council Bluffs behind. There had been a period in his earlier life when he would have yielded to the temptation to spend some time in the pleasure houses in the cities. But he was older now, and needed to complete this journey so as not to miss out on this opportunity to secure wealth untold.

John Wilson started life with the name John Cooper. He was Jennie Cooper's son, and had been dragged along by his saloon-girl mother as she traveled from town to town up and down the Mississippi River. River towns largely catered to a rough-and-tumble class of men made up of trappers, keel-boat operators, gamblers, and miners. Jennie had been pretty certain which trapper had made her pregnant with John, but Jacob was long gone by the time the child was born. Jennie and Jacob had never married. So the boy was given her surname, since no father would claim him. Miss Cooper made it clear to her son that she would be better off without him and couldn't wait for the day to come when he would be old enough to take care of himself.

Jennie never beat her boy, but occasionally one of her gentleman companions would trouble himself to give the lad a clout or a thrashing, if the mood struck him for any reason. He was forced to fend for himself or go hungry, so he developed his abilities for sneaking a little food for himself at an early age.

John plied his light-fingered skill frequently, always being careful never to take much—just what he needed to get by. He was not afraid to work, but few business owners were looking to hire a skinny fourteen-year-old who was the son of a known prostitute. Most women in whichever town they were living would not even talk to him or his mother.

Jennie and John had been in Galena, Illinois for much longer than they usually spent in one location. The lead ore in the area had drawn so many people to the settlement that its growth rivaled that of the city of Chicago one hundred-sixty miles east on the Lake Michigan shore.

When the town marshal of Galena, Illinois arrested a certain teen-aged thief for stealing dried apples from a barrel in a general store there, it was after seeing him do it on multiple other occasions. The lawman knew John's circumstances, and suggested John "try getting on with the Army." The marshal went so far as to suggest that Cooper go to Fort Armstrong on Rock Island to enlist. Though the garrison strength had been reduced there following the Black Hawk war, it was rumored that the Army was looking to add a few good riders to its cavalry troops due to the increased Indian activity west of the big river. John didn't bother to say good-bye to his mother. He knew she would not give a thought to him being gone, so he decided not to spend time finding her.

Traveling downriver was easy enough for John; he merely hitched a ride on a keelboat by agreeing to handle one of the long poles used for fending-off or propelling the boat. He arrived on the "big island" the following afternoon and walked through the gates of Fort Armstrong unchallenged.

That year had been 1839, and, as it turned out, the US Army did enlist young John Cooper as a cavalry trooper. He lied about his age, which was common enough, and the enlistment officer pretended not to notice the lad's lack of whiskers. At the time there was no way to prove that his surname was other than Wilson, which was the one he provided and used from that day forward.

For the next two decades, trooper John Wilson did as he was told and went where he was ordered. He saw parts of the nation that he might never have seen otherwise. He learned to obey men he disliked and disrespected. He learned to keep his mouth shut. He learned to hide his true feelings behind his wide, beaming grin. He became expert at wearing that smile when he would rather have beaten the person with his fists. He learned to spend long hours in a saddle as routine duty. In return, he was fed, clothed and sheltered. John survived his time in the Army in a near emotionless state. When he mustered out for the last time, he was equally unemotional. And he was superb at convincing people otherwise.

John Wilson met plenty of comrades-in-arms during those US Army years. Not all of his comrades‑ through the years shared his outlook on life, nor he theirs. But he knew who among them could be approached to enter into a profitable, if criminal, enterprise. The Kleins were three brothers from a small town called New Ulm in Minnesota, who had all returned to their home state when their enlistments expired in 1860, shortly before John himself left for Idaho Territory.

Now, in late September of 1863, John Wilson figured the time had come for him to pay a visit to his former comrades. As much as the Klein brothers had always shown an eagerness for gold, John reckoned they would be happy to join him in unloading a couple wagonloads of it. He needed to hurry so as to recruit his men and find the wagons before they crossed the Mississippi. John did some of his best and fastest riding ever as he cut across lands, some familiar, some unfamiliar to him. He occasionally laughed or smiled to himself, as thoughts of riches or dumb Irishmen crossed his mind.

\* \* \*

*Saturday, September 26, 1863. Larimer Street, outside the infamous Criterion Saloon, Denver, Colorado Territory.*

A Confederate sympathizer, obvious for his dirty grey Kepi-styled cap, called out to Billy in the middle of Larimer Street, "Whadya doin' in Denver, ya damned one-armed blue-belly? You got no business here." He was approaching the place where Billy stood alone. The aggressor's comrades on both his left and right seemed as eager as he to pick a fight with the disadvantaged former Union private, who happened to be wearing his blue sack coat against a cold spell that had come in that afternoon. From his slurred speech and difficulty maintaining his balance, the man was clearly drunk. His two friends were in similar condition. Still, three against one were unfair odds, multiplied by the fact of their intended victim having only one arm and no weapons. The other three all wore pistols holstered on their hips. Things didn't look good for the teen-aged former soldier from the North.

Patrick Murphy rounded the corner from 15th Street and saw Billy's predicament. He sprinted the short distance, gaining speed as he collided shoulder first with the bread basket of the main instigator, collapsing him into a gasping, wheezing heap. Billy dashed quickly to his left, engaging another of the thugs with a tightly clenched fist to the jaw, settling the matter for him. Patrick was up on his feet before the third troublemaker could manage to draw his gun from his holster. A fist to the mid-section followed by another to the point of the man's cheek just below his eye put him down and out. It was over before most witnesses were even sure what had taken place. Patrick and Billy gathered the pistols from the men on the ground, preventing the possibility of gunplay.

Two grey clad officers, in the uniforms of Confederate cavalry majors, burst forth from the door of the saloon and took up positions standing over the downed ruffians. The larger of the two majors hoisted the initiator of the trouble to his feet with one hand on the man's collar. Shaking him once for good measure, he asked, "What made you think that was a good idea?"

Still dazed and gasping for breath, his prisoner only shook his head in answer and tried to wrest himself free from the iron grip of his captor. Realizing the futility of his act, he abandoned it and shrugged, "We 'uz jes havin' a little fun with the blue-belly, Major. Nuthin' t' git upset about." His whiny, nasal tone annoyed Rob, reminding him of a more personal and deadly encounter he'd had the previous year in Kentucky.

"This is Colorado Territory! Not part of the war! Don't bring that trouble here, EVER! And don't forget it." Trembling with anger made the big Irishman appear all the more menacing to his listeners, especially the man he dropped back to the ground as he finished his statement. His face and eyes took on a fierceness that he seldom showed. The troublemaker and his companions were cowed by the exchange.

None of them replied nor even made eye contact when the tall major continued, "Gather your things and be gone from this city in one hour. No longer! If I see any of you or hear of your presence I will hunt you down, arrest you and turn you over to the law. Do you understand?"

All three of the men nodded and grunted their agreement. They stumbled to their feet as best they could, just in time to hear the Scottish accent of the other major, "And he'll not be alone in those pursuits, lads. You'd best clear off for yer own good." They heeded the warnings and advice by making as hasty a departure as they could.

Fortunately for Finn, Pinkerton, Walters, Murphy, and Adams, that was the end to the episode. There had been no follow-up by the town marshal, nor the US Marshal, nor any other officer of the law. It would most likely have been trouble had it turned out otherwise.

\* \* \*

When he had read Pinkerton's telegram a week earlier, Rob was caught completely by surprise. He could think of no reason why the agency owner would need to see him face-to-face. Once Pink arrived in Denver though, things became clear: Due to its nature, the current operational plans could not be put over the wire, and there had not been sufficient time for a letter to arrive. Thus Allan Pinkerton had acted as his own courier and messenger in this instance.

The Knights of the Golden Circle were stepping up their fundraising to sustain the Southern war efforts, sending out small groups of their most ardent members. They were intent on securing gold and silver to carry on the war. Two years into the fight, people and businesses of the South were disenchanted with any notion of a quick end to the conflict. They had no trust in the Confederate issued "greybacks" (the slang term for their paper currency), and were refusing to accept it in almost any quantity as payment.

For the South to continue fighting on would require more gold than what was being mined and minted in Georgia and New Mexico Territory. So, to finance the war to its conclusion, KCG leaders had their sights set on gold from the Colorado and Idaho Territories. Ore from those mining areas was assaying at higher values and being mined in greater quantities. Survival for their way of life, with or without the "peculiar institution" of slavery, depended upon the success of this goal. Labelling these teams of men "desperate" was no overstatement.

Though Allan Pinkerton was no longer officially head of military information for the Federal government, his personal relationship with Abraham Lincoln continued as before. Lincoln trusted Pinkerton and his spy organization to deliver essential military plans of the enemy. Congress had investigated Pinkerton's business dealings connected to services provided in the war effort because of the large amounts being paid to the Pinkerton Agency. As much as for any other reason, the Congressional committee insisted on cutting back such spending, "for appearances." Lincoln ordered his Treasury chief to use other means than those currently in use for paying the Pinkerton Agency. The President wanted to avoid further investigation or embarrassment. Secretary Chase had all Pinkerton invoice demands reimbursed with greenback dollars since they were much easier to manipulate than silver or gold coins.

While this change in payment methods seemed simple on the surface, it created problems for Pinkerton. He was already buying up both the US and and Confederate paper currencies at huge discounts–he had more of either than he wanted, but the discounts had been allowing him to multiply his buying power. With the supply of Federal gold into his business being effectively cut off by Secretary Chase's move, the Scot would lose much of his bargaining ability. Further, he had no desire to have large quantities of paper money. No one truly welcomed payments with the worthless notes, despite the US Congress declaring it legal tender. Merchants and tradesmen frowned on the stuff, and many were still insisting upon gold or silver coins for payment.

Arriving in town as quietly as possible under cover of darkness on Friday, September 25, Pinkerton had sent a sealed note to Finn's hotel by messenger. It had specified the time and place of their meeting, and that Rob should wear his Confederate major's uniform. Further, he was not to give his own name to anyone, so long as he could avoid it, and was not to inform any of his traveling cadre, other than Detective Walters, of the planned meeting. Rob would meet Pinkerton alone in the unofficial Confederate watering hole of Denver.

Their meeting in the Criterion Saloon next day was brief, and the only name attached to either of the uniformed men was that of Major E. J. Allen, CSA. Curiously enough, they both used the same name. This tactic was employed to deliberately confuse someone tracking Pinkerton's movements and to add a further red herring. Even Rob hadn't known in advance that Pinkerton would be attired in a uniform identical to his own, but knew enough not to bring up any topic while they were in the crowded tavern. This meeting would be according to Pinkerton's script, unless something unexpected came about.

Nothing unusual took place within the saloon. Several patrons cast approving looks at the two Southern cavalry officers, but everyone gave them plenty of privacy while they met. They had completed all of their brief business when loud voices from outside caught their attention. Rob recognized one of the voices and rose to his feet.

Upon spotting his two young companions' predicament, Finn acted to prevent further trouble. Pinkerton had admirably followed Finn's lead in the matter. Though their low-profiles were raised during the scuffle, it was a minimal exposure which could have been much worse. They adjourned to their separate hotels after Pinkerton quietly told Finn to expect another message.

Finn's guise as a Confederate officer was ruined, but only with Patrick and Billy. They hurried back to the hotel, where he explained more about himself than he had intended. Rob stated forcefully the importance of maintaining his Pinkerton job and his alternate identity as secrets. His life, their lives, and others depended upon it at times. Both Murphy and Adams agreed to keep the information to themselves.

Waiting in his hotel room two hours later, Finn had Pink's message in hand. Pinkerton directed Finn and Walters to meet with him in the dining room of their hotel wearing civilian clothes. He further instructed Finn and Walters to refer to the agency head only by his given name, Allan, and to bring no one else to this meeting. Naturally Finn and Walters complied with these instructions.

Having just spent time with Pinkerton earlier the same day, Finn was impressed by the simple steps his boss had taken to make himself less recognizable. A padded vest added at least thirty pounds to the Scot's appearance. He was wearing a pair of eyeglasses as well. These two elements of costuming were surprisingly effective.

Once they had ordered their dinners and gotten down to the details of business, there were several more unexpected revelations. Pinkerton admitted that the increased issuance of paper money was destroying the confidence of Lincoln's wealthy political backers. What the administration was now bargaining and trading with was land grants, especially to the railroad companies, something Lincoln understood well. He and his administration were using lands taken from the Indians to advance the fortunes of a few wealthy groups in order to finance the North's war costs.

Though he continued to be a firm opponent of the practice of one man owning another, Pinkerton confessed that he saw the long-term indebtedness being perpetrated upon the citizens by the manipulation of currencies and financial instruments as being another form of slavery. His point being that it made no sense to trade one form of slavery for another, especially at the expense of so much physical suffering, death, and property loss. He pressed both Finn and Walters for assurances that neither would ever share his positions with others on this matter. Both nodded their solemn assurances, before Pinkerton went even further.

Pinkerton explained that the President had a natural aversion to the bloodshed and hatred being unleashed by the war. Lincoln even feared that, rather than holding the nation together, it might tear things apart irreparably for generations to come. Publicly, Lincoln seemed the cool, collected Commander-in-Chief requiring his generals to send men into harm's way to win battles at whatever cost. Privately, Lincoln agreed more with McClellan's conservative approach to battle. In replacing McClellan with Grant, Lincoln had yielded to both political and public pressure. While it had appeased many who clamored for a more aggressive pursuit, the action had also shown that Lincoln could be influenced by the opinions of others. McClellan was not the only permanent enemy the President earned in taking this action.

Then there was the matter of the Secretary of the Treasury to discuss, Salmon P. Chase, whose political ambitions included the Presidency. His policies as head of the Treasury were effective in keeping the Federal government solvent. Though he didn't favor the unbacked paper notes, he saw their issuance as a necessary means to an end. Therefore he oversaw the issuance and printing of the greenbacks with his usual firm hand. His view on the prosecution of the war, and its battles, favored harshness and brashness.

Chase saw in his role as Treasury Chief an opportunity to build a vast network of agents across the western territories in addition to the northern states. These agents were loyal only to the Treasury Department, ultimately to Chase, and became his own small army for conducting operations as he saw fit. Secretary Chase and President Lincoln were political adversaries who barely tolerated one another. So much so, that Chase had given Lincoln letters of resignation on several occasions; each was refused because the President saw the nation's need of Chase's advice and connections.

Such were the complexities of these issues in Washington, D.C. that Pinkerton had legitimate concerns regarding the continuation of his agency's relationship with the Federal government. In confessing these details to his two detectives, Allan Pinkerton was making himself and his plans vulnerable. All three men knew the personal stakes were high for the agency owner.

At the mention of the amount of gold being produced from the Pinkerton Agency claim in Bannack, Pinkerton brightened and asked if the two men would take ownership of the claim directly as partial payment for their ongoing service. It was a generous offer of compensaton that would also circumvent some of the difficulties with finances going on in the Federal capital. Seeing the wisdom in this, both the field detectives accepted willingly.

When Finn and Walters finished the details of their activity reports to their employer, Finn added their opinion that the Treasury Department might not return the gold stolen by Treasury Agent Emry to its rightful owners. He further outlined a simple plan to bypass St. Louis, bringing the Bannack gold straight into Chicago, then handling the return to rightful owners as a function of and under the protection of the Pinkerton Agency. Pinkerton immediately expressed his liking for the idea, encouraging his two men to share completely what they had in mind. Finn and Walters shared their thoughts; Pinkerton added a few ideas of his own. At the end of their time sketching out ideas and plans, Pinkerton re-stated his two key themes.

"I've no doubt that we'll have our hands full, trying to keep those Treasury boys from interferin', even if we do manage to bypass St. Louis. We have to remember our main goal is to keep as much gold as possible from falling into the wrong hands. That has always been, and should always be, our foremost consideration. And knowing which are the wrong hands is key to the survival of this country."

Rob and Lonnie nodded their understanding. They could not have agreed more with Pinkerton's last statement. Both were dedicated to keeping gold from falling into the wrong hands.

# CHAPTER EIGHT

# River Crossings

*The first week of October 1863, Nebraska Territory, along the southern bank of the Platte River.*

Though they all would have been happier had the pace of their travel been faster, they had managed to average over twenty-five miles per day and there had not been a single incident nor accident since leaving Denver. With the large, wide wheels on their wagons, the teams pulling them were doing well against the heavy loads each carried. But doing well did not include great speed. They knew that their slow-moving train was an easy target tempting any who wanted to test their luck.

Colorado Territory and most of Nebraska Territory were behind them, and their Union military escort surrounded them. If things continued to go well, the group driving their gold shipments eastward would be crossing into the State of Iowa soon. Iowa being a settled state brought about a sense of relief to all of them. Rob was grateful for the help Pinkerton had provided in mapping their trek eastward. He was equally aware of how much help the Mormons had provided to them and all east-west travelers. Mormon river-crossing markers, road signs, and camping places, all of which were established during members of that religion's travels a score of years earlier made things much easier for the gold haulers.

Rob was still carrying the two telegraphed messages that Crisman had handed to him on his last day in Bannack. That had already been over a month ago. Neither message was entirely composed of bad or good news. The first was from Maggie stating:

**Fine in Delavan. John ran off with circus.**

Rob was neither particularly surprised nor troubled by the news. John could handle himself well and the circus people would feed him and look after him. That Maggie made no mention of other trouble was a good sign.

His other telegram was from a member of the Mabie Circus, informing Mr. Robert Finn, via the Pinkerton Agency, Chicago that:

**Young John saved the day. Return Delavan December 1.**

Puzzled by this message from one Stewart Craven, Rob decided that perhaps things were working out for the best. If he could not be present to referee the difficulties between his wife and son, it might be best that they be apart. The fact that a man had taken the trouble and spent the money to notify him about his young son was comforting. He may have been more concerned, had he known all the details.

Young John had indeed saved the day during an incident that had taken place in August. The circus's big elephant, Romeo, had trapped his trainer, Stewart Craven, in a corner of the training cage they were working in while in Minneapolis, Minnesota. John's quick thinking and action to throw a stool at the enraged elephant, distracting the beast, had undoubtedly save the trainer's life. Everyone in the circus was talking about it. Rob would not know the details for some time to come. The incident was witnessed by a local newspaper reporter, and the article he posted describing the raging giant elephant, coupled with the courage of the young handler brought in new waves of curious circus-goers. The Mabie Brothers show was invited to stay on for two more weeks in Minneapolis.

Meanwhile, Rob had sent a telegram to Maggie from Denver assuring her that he was fine, and that he'd heard from John who also seemed to be well. He added that he hoped to be home by the end of October. Rob's message to his wife read:

**Fine in Denver. John fine Minneapolis. Home**
**November 1**

He added,

**Devoted, R.F.**

as his sign-off to his message. She was his wife, after all.

The two youngest members of the group, Patrick and Billy, felt greater confidence in their ability to handle themselves since the confrontation that had taken place outside the Criterion Saloon in Denver a few days before leaving the city. Such confidence is often the province of young men following a recent fight in which they had been victorious. It was not wisdom to expect all future outcomes to turn out so well. The escort and the wagon drivers were all aware of this fact. They did not allow their slight sense of relief to lull them into thinking that nothing could go wrong. There were plenty of miles and plenty of crossings ahead.

* * *

*Friday, October 9, 1863. New Ulm, Minnesota.*

John Wilson knew things were going his way upon finding all three of the Klein brothers at home when he arrived in New Ulm, Minnesota. Not only were they home, but their farm chores were completed for the harvest or else nearly so. They excitedly embraced his plan to enrich themselves when Wilson laid out how they could relieve Finn and Walters of the gold they were transporting. They were ready to leave the following Tuesday.

These four former US Cavalry troopers were hell-bent on personal riches now, however gotten. The Kleins explained to Wilson that the government was paying a twenty-five dollar bounty per scalp for each adult male Sioux Indian. Both Federal and State of Minnesota governments had decided upon this method to bring an end to what they deemed "the Indian problem." In their heightened state of greed, the brothers pointed out that there would still be plenty of small parties of Sioux around, and declared that "the real harvest had just begun."

Figuring they could each collect between five and ten Sioux scalps every day as they rode south through Minnesota and Iowa, they were counting the number of "thousand dollar days" that lay between New Ulm and Dubuque. Their increasingly coarse laughter told that greed was stoking a powerful evil within each of the men. They could not wait to begin killing for profit. John Wilson was as caught up by the planned blood-lust as the brothers, despite his closeness with numerous Indians. There was no longer any rational, ethical behavior or thinking going on in the man. In his mind, it was time for him get his share, and he would not be denied.

*  *  *

*Friday, October 9, 1863. Late morning, about three miles west of Plattsmouth, Nebraska Territory.*

As the wagons traveled along carrying their golden cargos, the sounds of the river off to the trail's north side were those common to any large river. However, drinking water drawn from the Platte River needed time for all the fine silt suspended in it to settle. And extra care had to be taken when watering the animals or gathering water from the sloughs along its banks. The Platte River was known for its quicksand and, more recently, an increase in hostile

Indian activity along some of the reaches on the northern side. That they had covered so many miles without seeing even a small hunting party was a relief. An Indian attack was less likely with each passing mile. Now the likelihood of trouble from either bushwhackers, Red Legs, or KGC members would increase until crossing the Mississippi. And they needed to get their heavily loaded wagons across the Missouri River before worrying about the Mississippi.

Another of their carefully chosen options was to cross the Missouri River at the small city of Plattsmouth, avoiding the need to cross the Platte River at all. They would miss Omaha and Council Bluffs, but were well-enough provisioned that no real need to pass through those cities existed. And according to their overall plan, the fewer pairs of eyes viewing their trek eastward, the better. Regular ferry service was available at Plattsmouth and steamboat traffic was frequent enough that they found a side-wheeler with room for all three wagons as soon as they arrived at the docks.

Towering high over their heads, the double-decked ship did not so much as tremble when the crowds of people boarded. Even their heavy wagons and mule teams made no difference in the way the huge vessel sat in the water as they loaded. Crossing the Missouri River and disembarking was without incident; then they were traveling across Iowa.

While yet together as a train of three wagons, they would continue to traverse Iowa's southern counties until reaching their intended crossing of the Des Moines River at the small town of Pittsburg. This would be their last fording of a major river. All other crossings were planned to be on barges, ferries, steamboats, or via railroad cars crossing a man-made bridge. Such were the marvels of modern engineering. The company would be breaking up just beyond the east side of the Des Moines River.

Although he believed their planning of routes had been sound, Rob was still harboring concerns for the safety of the two wagons that would be taking the more northerly of the three routes. Both would be without the military escort detail and traveling alone after parting at the small crossroads town of New Philadelphia, Iowa.

* * *

*Tuesday, October 13, 1863. East Bank of the Des Moines River, Van Buren County, Iowa.*

It had been nine weeks since Jenkins, Murphy, and Adams left St. Louis on the road west. For this stretch of his return journey, Jenks' would now follow the Des Moines river southeast to its junction with the Mississippi at Keokuk. After crossing there, he and his military escort would then travel southward to St. Louis on the Illinois side as additional precaution against attack. Before re-crossing into the State of Missouri, the Treasury

Department would meet them opposite St. Louis with a specially-armored wagon for the final move of the coins into the city. The wagon driven by Jenkins would have the full military escort all the way to his destination–which was a relief to Rob and Lonnie regarding the man's safety. This was another of the planned details to avoid traffic as well as any eyes watching for such a shipment arriving from Denver.

Patrick Murphy and Billy Adams had formed friendships with Jenks during their time together. They took time to say proper good-byes before turning with Rob and Lonnie to take the northern-most track of the three wagons. When the last of the parting good-byes had been spoken, Jenks turned his team to the southeast and let this whip gently pop over the heads of his veteran mule team as he let out his customary, "High on!" The wagon pulled away smoothly and swiftly with the mounted military escort maintaining formation while keeping up with their charge.

While the Jenks wagon was yet disappearing in the dust and the distance, the two northbound wagons continued on in company for another full day. On the morning of Thursday, October 15, 1863, these wagons separated for the last time at a crossroad west of the river town called Muscatine on the Mississippi River's western bank. Finn and Walters exchanged goodbyes with Babcock and Thatcher. These four had also been riding and working together for about nine weeks. A major difference in the partings was that the two Military Information operatives and the two Pinkerton Detectives had reason to believe they would likely see each other in the future.

The two men with the load destined for Chicago turned to the right. A remaining soldier from the Colorado contingent, dressed in civilian clothing, would accompany this wagon to its final destination. Pinkerton had helped arrange this small detail with the authorities in Denver, adding that it was "sensitive agency business" which created the need. No further details of that need were given.

Babcock and Thatcher would spend a day or two at Thatcher's family farm outside Muscatine, before crossing by flatboat, ferry, or steamboat at their option. Their wagon was similar enough to a heavy farm wagon that it would raise no eyebrows along the farmlands of their planned route or crossing.

Then, after arriving in Illinois, Babcock, Thatcher and their companion would travel north to the town of Colona, where they would arrange transport for their wagon to Chicago via rail. If boxcar accommodations were available on the Chicago and Rock Island Rail Road, they would bring their mules with. If not, they were prepared to sell the team to a local livery, even if they had to accept a sacrifice price. Several times Babcock wondered how much of a hullabaloo would be raised when the wagon he was responsible for reached Chicago. Treasury

Department officials in St. Louis were bound to be angry about the unauthorized re-routing.

Finn and Walters would drive their wagon much further north along the west side of the Mississippi. They would take care to avoid the Davenport and Rock Island area. Heavy police and military presence in those cities outweighed the convenience of crossing the river by bridge. Since Murphy and Adams were with them, there seemed no need for additional escort riders.

Their further plan called for the Finn-Walters party crossing the Mississippi at the city of Dubuque, Iowa. From there they would drive the heavy circus wagon, (now painted a pleasing shade of forest green), to Freeport, where it would be loaded onto the train for final off-loading at Delavan, Wisconsin.

\* \* \*

*Thursday, October 15, 1863. On the road south of Little Warsaw, Illinois*

Jenks and his traveling escort crossed the Mississippi River easily, boarding a huge stern-wheeler at Keokuk, Iowa, which landed less than an hour later at the Little Warsaw wharf on the Illinois side. Total time to load, cross and disembark was less than three hours. The wagon, the driver, the mules, the military escort and their mounts made the crossing without so much as drawing a sharp breath of concern in the process. After Jenks was satisfied that his mule team was properly fitted into their traces, the whole company moved off with no fanfare. No one paid attention to the mounted soldiers accompanying the wagon. There was a war going on and people had become accustomed to seeing uniformed men moving round.

*Saturday, October 17, 1863. After breakfast on the northbound road,west of Davenport, Iowa.*

Lonnie sensed Rob's edginess while they were breaking camp after breakfast this morning. It was still dark, which was common for their day's start, but this was different. They had driven for several hours longer than was usual on each of the last two days, since parting with Babcock and Thatcher. Rob was pushing himself and others harder to make more miles before stopping for the day. Lonnie had had to mention twice last evening that this was wearing out their mule team. Finn finally yielded after the second time Walters mentioned it. But it was very unlike Finn not to heed Walters' advice about the animals.

"Sorry about the rush, Lonnie, an' for the mood along with it. Ah don't know why, but Ah've got the strongest feeling that somethin's not right an' we need to get across this river soon. It's strange ... Ah can't explain it." Rob's confession came about almost as though he had read Lonnie's thoughts of a few moments earlier.

*Saturday, October 17, 1863. Mid-morning in the middle of the Mississippi River, just below the downriver end of Hog Island.*

Asa Thatcher's parents had been only too happy when their son and his two traveling companions arrived on Thursday afternoon to spend two nights in the family home. The Thatchers enjoyed entertaining guests on those few occasions that they had them; it was a special treat that one of them was their own son. They seldom heard from Asa since he had enlisted and this was the first time he had been home in longer than they could remember. Asa's younger brother and sister were so excited to see their big brother they couldn't sleep the first night of his visit.

Explaining only that he and his two companions were traveling to Chicago on Treasury Department business, Asa assured his family he would stop back as soon as he was able, but that he would have to make crossing arrangements on Friday and leave Saturday morning. Mrs. Thatcher fussed a little about the shortness of the visit; Mr. Thatcher, Asa, Sr., was more accepting of his son's duty to his government position.

In any event, the visit had passed quickly, more so since it took several hours on Friday to arrange two flat-bottomed barges for their Saturday crossing. The river was low enough that the current was less than during times of higher water, and there were no snags to be seen. The

Charles White father-and-son ferry-operating team had gone across and back on Thursday and assured them there was no problem with their heavy wagon and mule team on their barges.

An inspection of the two river-craft showed them to be large enough and sturdy enough to Asa's practiced eye. He would have preferred that they cross on one of the steam-powered boats; Babcock argued that the service they were hiring was a better fit with their travel schedule and that the price was much less. Though he didn't bring it up, Babcock was the senior member of their team, so the decision was his if he claimed it. Thatcher agreed before it got to that point. Asa realized he might have been harboring a stubborn preference due to his liking for steam engines and being around them.

Their young soldier companion had remained quiet during the discussion, having nothing to contribute. He was not anxious to share his fear of the big river nor the fact that he could not swim. It embarrassed him that he was afraid, so he was determined not to let the others see his fear. And whether he was fearful or not, the group would board these two barges and cross the river tomorrow. Caleb Agnew, for that was his name, guessed correctly that he would not sleep that night, being so worried about the crossing.

Loading the wagon and the mules onto the two barges that morning went smoothly. The team backed the wagon onto the first barge and then stood patiently while they were unhitched. Then it was their turn to be loaded onto the second barge, the one on which Caleb would ride and the younger White would captain. Caleb was relieved to be riding with the mules and the younger oarsman for the crossing. His stomach was churning so much he thought he might lose this morning's breakfast at any time. At least the Treasury Department agents wouldn't see or hear him retching if it came to that.

With the October wind whipping down across the water, the men were glad to have bundled into heavy coats before saying goodbye to the Thatchers after breakfast. Asa's mother encouraged her son to "hurry back, and bring friends along any time, including the nice Mr. Babcock and Mr. Agnew." The woman was capable of making strangers feel welcome at her table even as she bid them goodbye.

Asa, Sr. extended his arm and shook hands with his departing guests. His strong grip left no doubt that he was well-acquainted with hard work. And his sincere smile and gracious words, "Don't let it be so long before we see you next," reminded his son how much he loved his parents. In that bittersweet moment Asa, Jr. made a firm promise to himself to return to Muscatine as soon as he could. Permanently. This really was his home.

Waves lapped against the upstream sides of the two boats as they navigated the mid-stream channel. They were not so high as to soak the passengers or cargo of the two boats. It was more that they acted as reminders to all aboard that the wind and water were their masters while they rode among them.

The Upper Mississippi River had been challenging white settlers' schemes and plans for decades. Various parties of surveyors and engineers had studied the upper reaches of the waterway above St. Louis. The main channel of the river shifted and changed daily and weekly due to the high silt content it carried along and the varying currents and eddies caused by snags and other submerged object moving along the bottom. Sounding and reading the river were two occupations being constantly employed by those who made their living from carrying traffic on or across its hazardous surface.

Not far from the location of today's crossing at Muscatine, two very different people had played significant roles in the nation's progress to tame the Mississippi. One of them, a young army engineering lieutenant and West Point graduate by the name of Robert E. Lee, had helped map the dangerous rapids in the Rock Island stretch of the river in 1837. Lee also devised a plan for building a canal to make the river navigable for large vessels through the Des Moines rapids downriver in the Keokuk area.

The other man was a lawyer representing the Rock Island Railroad Company in the 1856 lawsuit brought against the railroad for damages to a steamboat that collided with their bridge at Rock Island. The railroad won the case in 1857, which aided further and more rapid expansion of the westward building of railroads. That lawyer's name was Abraham Lincoln, and the case brought national attention to both the issue and the man.

Babcock and Thatcher had every confidence in the bargemen handling the big sweeps on the heavily-loaded boats. They were experienced oarsmen of well-built and well-maintained craft. Thatcher was favorably impressed with the care and skill the father-and-son team and their hired men showed when loading and lashing the wagon and the mule team. He again acknowledged their skill when he observed the way the two boats were maneuvered around Hog Island. These men and craft had crossed the river two days before in this same channel. All the indicators were favorable for a safe, incident-free trip.

No one knows, nor can anyone predict why a "deadhead" snag loosens or rises in a river just when it does so. This, coupled with the fact that they are hidden several feet below the muddy surface of the river is what makes them so lethally dangerous to river traffic. Asa Thatcher and Charles White both spotted the rising monster at the same moment and shouted as one, "Hold on!" A split second later the huge tree trunk had ripped a gash nine feet long and half as wide in the bottom of the vessel transporting the freight wagon. At the same time, the log pushed the hull up more than two feet out of the water before sinking down to the riverbed again. The result was disastrous beyond imagining.

The damaged barge began to sink immediately, listing to the upstream side where the snag had smashed into the hull. Being so heavily loaded and lashed to the deck, the wagon contributed to the speed at which the boat capsized. Such rapid and powerful churning threw everyone off balance, physically and emotionally. Babcock found himself in the chilly current trying to tread water while wearing soaked, heavy clothing. He could swim a little in normal conditions, but coughed violently and gasped for air when he came up after the unexpected submersion. His eyes flashed pure panic when he saw the last part of the wagon disappear below the murky river water.

Babcock's panic had nothing to do with the loss of the precious cargo they'd been carrying. It was the product of his sudden realization that he could actually drown right here. Just as his arms started to flail the water a large arm and hand gripped his neck and shoulder, pinching tightly even through the thick layers of his clothing. He was being dragged, forcefully, through the water toward the barge carrying the mules. And he was grateful to be above water, whoever was rescuing him.

Asa's long, powerful strokes brought Babcock to the remaining barge swiftly, where two sets of hands hoisted him from the water. Thatcher was swimming back to the place the wagon and barge had slipped beneath the waves. While the others had made it safely to the other barge, one of the ferrymen was yet missing. Charles White had somehow become entangled in the ropes lashing the wagon to the boat and gone down with the cargo. Asa

Thatcher dove once, staying down trying to free the struggling boatman; then his own breath was gone. He began to pass out. When Thatcher's head broke the surface again it took him several moments to get his bearings and clear his mind. His strength was sapping away from the cold and exertion.

Taking several deep breaths before holding the last of them in, Thatcher dove once more to where he thought the victim would be, but found nothing. He was again nearing the end of his available air when his hand brushed the unmistakeable feel of a human face. Asa followed the body down to where the rope was tightened around White's ankle. He never knew where he got the strength to do so at this point in the struggle, but he grasped the rope with both hands and pulled for all he was worth. Somehow the heavy line parted.

A moment later, Asa Thatcher was again on the surface gasping for breath, holding Charles White, Sr. under the chin and dragging him to the nearby island of safety–the other barge. White was unconscious or worse. Pairs of strong hands pulled White and Thatcher from the water. Asa did not have the strength left to crawl further onto the deck of the boat.

All the activity and excitement had spooked the mules. Young Caleb Agnew rose to the occasion, calming his own fears while helping to calm the animals. He continued his soothing talk and stroking as he passed among them and stayed out of the way of the others who were tending to the tasks of getting the barge off the river and reviving Charles White, Sr. White had been turned on his side and slapped soundly on the back, then rolled onto his chest and thumped a few more times. After finally turning the unconscious man onto his back, his son and one of the hired ferrymen began working his arms in a fashion to restore the function of breathing.

Following an abrupt coughing up of water, the elder White gasped, coughed some more, then began breathing again. Soon he was sitting upright, huddled with the other passengers (including Thatcher and Babcock) surrounded by the standing mules, wrapped in combinations of canvas, blankets, and whatever other dry materials were available. Their shivering lessened before they reached the Illinois shore, and conversations laced with 'Thank you's" were heard before anyone set foot on the eastern bank of the deadly river.

Asa Thatcher, Jr. kept his thoughts to himself. He had never been so terrified before in his life. The river's power, which he thought he understood, had surpassed all his previous thoughts of its might. His was now the respect born of near-death experience which resulted in a greater wisdom just afterward.

Those who had not been immersed by the incident handled the unloading of the mule team and what gear survived the sinking. There was not much of a town grown up on the east bank of the river. Once they stepped off the wharf, Babcock and Thatcher were faced with some immediate decisions. Should they try to venture on to Colona per the original plan, or send a telegram and find someplace to stay while awaiting further orders? What about the shipment of gold now tumbling along the bottom of the Mississippi River? What could be done about that?

Babcock opted to send telegrams addressed to the Pinkerton Agency and to Rob Finn in Dubuque, knowing that Finn might be elsewhere. At least this way, Rob would be notified of a message when he checked into a telegraph office. Pinkerton would know of the incident almost at once. The agency owner had left Denver ahead of the wagons by a couple of days. His travel via the Overland Stage route would have been faster and much more direct. Babcock imagined that Pinkerton was most likely in St. Louis, possibly already back in Washington, D.C. That the Treasury Department or others would also receive the telegraphed information could not be helped.

The accommodating owner of a small tavern and inn on the east-west road leading inland from the wharf area offered to arrange sending either a messenger back across the river to send telegrams or a rider north to Moline for the same purpose. A unanimous decision to send the rider north arose from the throats of those who had just witnessed or experienced a near-drowning. None, including the ferrymen, were anxious to send anyone over the Mississippi just yet. It was the innkeeper's own son who rode north to the telegraph office in Moline.

\* \* \*

*Wednesday, October 21, 1863. Sunset over Dubuque, Iowa, from a hilltop west of the city.*

Since the skirmish with the Sioux warriors that resulted in the woundings or death of every member of the Wilson-Klein gang, John Wilson had been traveling alone. Both he and his horse needed medical treatment, but he was reluctant to enter the city before darkness set in. There would be some residents here that disapproved of hunting scalps in Minnesota, so he would keep to the shadows until he found the help he needed. The lone scalp he had collected during this ill-conceived venture was certainly not worth the trouble. He was mentally scolding himself for his stupidity, and worse, for getting caught up in such a scheme.

Wilson worried his hip was infected, and Xander, his faithful mount, was favoring his injured right hind leg. The bow of just one Sioux warrior had dealt those arrow-inflicted wounds to both John and his horse, before Wilson's final bullet fired from his repeating carbine stilled the hands holding that bow.

Two of the Kleins had been killed outright in the first encounter, when the four overeager scalp-hunters surprised themselves and a small Sioux hunting party by carelessly galloping over the top of a ridge right into the tribal group. That had beenon the second day out of New

Ulm, as their course veered easterly before heading straight south again into Iowa. Wilson and the third Klein brother escaped immediate extinction by sheer luck.

That luck ended abruptly with an arrow between Hans Klein's shoulders that took him off his horse, which then continued galloping on riderless. Wilson's right hip caught an arrow, as did Xander's. Both arrows went deep into the flesh. Xander managed a final sprint into a heavily wooded ravine at Wilson's urging. No pursuers followed them into it.

John Wilson circled back many hours later on foot, in the dark. That trip was excruciatingly slow. He paused with each step to listen. When he finally reached the vicinity of the last exchange of fire between the opposing forces, he was reduced to searching on his hands and knees. Klein might have crawled into cover anywhere, and even now might have a gun pointed in the direction of any sound Wilson made. Should he call out?

The question of how best to find the wounded man answered itself when Wilson stumbled over the man's corpse. Judging by the location and its position, it seemed clear that the arrow had killed him. Klein's scalp had been taken, though he probably never felt it. Wilson shuddered at the memory. Scalping was a fear he had lived with all his days as a cavalry trooper. Now he himself had become guilty of scalping another human being.

It was five days since he left the cover of that ravine. Following the Turkey River southeast helped him avoid others while providing the most direct route to Dubuque. It had been slow going through the State of Iowa. Walking was all Wilson or his horse could manage; limping along at that.

During those days, he had been thinking up a story to tell Finn. He was still determined to get some of the gold for himself, but his earlier plan to attack the wagon en route would no longer work. A new approach was needed. Wilson was disgusted with himself for not having come up with this idea sooner. He had never needed the Kleins– should never have involved them in his plans. At least now he wouldn't have to share his profits with the brothers. Since he was already friendly with Finn and Walters, no explanation about additional companions would be necessary. Yes. This new plan was better all the way 'round: safer, smarter, and he might not need to kill anyone else.

\* \* \*

*Wednesday, October 21st, 1863. Just before sunset, headed north into Dubuque up the final incline to the crest of the hill west of the city.*

As they rode along, Rob was gazing ahead into the farthest distances his sight could probe. It was almost as if he were trying to see into the future. Lonnie was driving, Patrick was riding Bricks while Billy rode Roxie. Their pace was leisurely, as it had been during the entire ride northward since parting with Babcock and Thatcher outside Muscatine. They were nearing a point on the road where it would descend to the city of Dubuque below along the Mississippi River. Crossing the next day was their intention.

"Stop the wagon, Lonnie!" Rob's blurted command brought the other three from their lulled states of mind. Finn was already jumping down from the seat. He hit the ground moving toward Murphy and Bricks. His next shouted order was for Patrick to dismount Bricks. An instant later he was riding the black horse up the grade to where a figure, barely visible in the growing dusk, stood holding the reins to a horse.

"John Wilson!" Finn's exclamation was a combination of surprise and puzzlement at seeing the man he had not expected to see for many months, perhaps a year or more, if ever.

Equally surprised by the timing of this chance meeting, Wilson had hurriedly finished composing the tale he would tell Finn to account for his presence and circumstances. Mustering up his broadest grin, Wilson looked Rob in the eyes and said calmly, "You sure are a sight for these sore eyes, Rob Finn. You won't believe all that's happened since I left Denver."

Finn made a rapid assessment of the condition of the horse and rider, and suggested they stand easy while the wagon drove up to them. Lonnie braked the wagon at the top of the incline and made the traces fast to the brake lever before climbing down. He also greeted Wilson cheerily in the fashion of those who had been through trials and labors together. Murphy and Adams, who knew Wilson only from short encounters with him in Denver, were friendly though not entirely engaged in the re-union going on.

Darkness was upon the hilltop gathering before Wilson could satisfy all their questions with detailed answers. Walters had done the briefest of examinations of Wilson's hip, as well as Xander's. The look he gave Rob told the story. They both needed treatment and sooner would be best. Wilson was loaded into the wagon where he could recline for further examination and treatment by Walters, while Xander's saddle was removed and stowed. Lonnie climbed into the living quarters of the big wagon to attend to Wilson's wound.

Patrick Murphy assured Rob that he could handle the wagon in response to Rob's question, and Billy would continue to accompany the wagon as it slowly found its way down into the darkness of the valley. Billy would ride just ahead as a look-out, since Patrick would have his hands full driving the mule team on the downgrade. They lit the lamps, hanging the smaller one within the cabin of the wagon and the larger coach lamp on the post by the driver's seat. It was a godsend that the road bed was well-built and maintained on a gentle downgrade.

With arrangements being the best they could do for the moment, Rob rode off into the dark, telling his companions that he would be in search of a doctor, and a horse doctor, and the telegraph office. He'd also told them to meet him at the Hotel Julien on the corner of Main and Second streets. Being the largest building downtown would make it easy to find. He told them anything else that needed attending to would have to wait.

Rob and Bricks loped gently down the hill several hundred yards before he reigned the big horse around to his right and lead him off the roadway. He dismounted and walked slowly down the incline well beyond where light from the wagon would have any effect. Calming Bricks with a low, soothing voice while stroking a cheek with a hand, they waited, keeping absolute quiet, while the wagon rolled on down the hill toward the city. Rob walked the pair slowly back the way they had come. After reaching the road again, and making certain he was well out of sight from the wagon, he remounted Bricks. Together they returned to the top of the hill where they had first caught up with Wilson.

Finn again dismounted. Walking slowly and carefully, he traveled in increasingly larger circles from the point he estimated Wilson to have been standing when Rob first encountered him. It didn't take long to find the object he was looking for: a recently obtained human scalp. Wilson had tossed it away while Rob was approaching earlier. He also found two crumpled pieces of paper, which he picked up and pocketed. It was too dark to read them, but he was pretty certain that, in the light of day, he would recognize the handwriting as his own.

If he had any doubts about Wilson earlier, there were none lingering any longer.

\* \* \*

The gas lamps at Dubuque's major downtown intersections were already lit when Rob rode up to the parked wagon. A quick survey revealed that the wagon was empty and he could see Roxie hitched just ahead of the mule team. He crossed quickly into the main entrance of the luxury hotel. His group was huddled around Wilson, who was seated on one of the hotel's beautiful chairs in the main lobby area. The concierge was making notes and talking with Walters when Rob arrived. Finn overheard the other man speaking to Lonnie.

"Well, no, sir, he is not a surgeon, but he is highly regarded in this city for his skill and acumen regarding all things pharmacological. Doctor Mason has been practicing in Dubuque for nigh onto thirty years." It was obvious the concierge was himself an educated man and confident regarding the medical man he was recommending. Finished with his explanation, the man turned to Rob, as did Lonnie.

"Mr. Finlay, this is Rob Finn, who I was telling you about," Lonnie began his introduction. "Rob, this is young

Mr. Finlay, son of one of the hotel's owners. He assures me that he can have Doctor Timothy Mason on the premises to look at Wilson's injuries within the hour. The hotel has sufficient room for our entire group, and their livery service can see to our wagon and animals, including Wilson's horse." Walters was using his best English and diction. These surroundings, The Hotel Julien's extravagant and elegant furnishings, decorations, and style had that affect on people. Finn noted that Patrick and Billy were looking about sheepishly. Neither had ever seen, let alone been in, such grandeur before. None of them were dressed for their surroundings and the dust from the road covered them all.

Various members of the hotel's staff were already seeing to the travelers' needs: two bellmen had gone out to the wagon to retrieve what bags Lonnie and Patrick directed, another two were helping Wilson up the grand staircase, liverymen were summoned to take the wagon and the animals into the shelter of the barn. All this was before Rob had even brought out gold coins to pay for the services. He and Pinkerton had stayed in the Hotel Julien once, and it was living up to its impeccable reputation as well as his memory of the place. Despite the shabbiness of the traveling company's appearance, all members of the staff treated each of them as politely and graciously as though they were royalty.

As promised, Doctor Mason arrived soon after they were established in their rooms. The man exuded confidence, intelligence, and experience, yet was as gentle in his words and mannerisms toward his patient as he was skillful in his ministrations. Lonnie was favorably impressed by all these goings on as was plain to see from his nodding agreements and the look on his face. Doctor Mason complimented Walters for having scrubbed and bathed the wound and applying the home-made tincture of iodine that Lonnie showed him.

Finally, after Wilson had swallowed a generous dose of laudanum and fallen into the sleep of someone heavily drugged, the doctor departed, promising to come back the next morning. He advised Walters and Finn that Wilson "might be a little out of his head" and talk nonsense, and that it was nothing to be concerned with.

All the while that the doctor had been attending his patient, members of the hotel staff had been coming and going, taking orders for food and beverages, then delivering them to the correct patrons in turn.

Billy and Patrick were wide-eyed with excitement at the goings on and the delicious nature of the foods they received. They grinned like small boys with each bite of some new and delicious concoction they sampled. In their minds, if this place was not heaven, it must be awfully close to it.

Every member of the group enjoyed the luxurious food and other amenities the hotel provided. It seemed that everything was simply the best. In the mornings they could dine in style in the dining room or enjoy fresh pastries with their coffee and a newspaper in the lobby or even in their rooms. Rob and Lonnie scoured the newspapers daily for items of interest. They were especially looking for any mention of the goings on out west. Rob thought he had found something when a headline mentioning a cougar caught his attention. It turned out to be nothing, though. Occasionally one of the big cats would turn up locally. Announced sightings would terrify the women and children for a while and then the animal would disappear again, and all would be forgotten until the next sighting.

Rob and Lonnie agreed they would not be forgetting the Hotel Julien's coffee and pastry for a long time to come.

* * *

*Monday, October 26, 1863. A wooded and sheltered ravine just north and west of Dubuque, Iowa. The full moon is high in the cloudless sky.*

Following the white man had been easy enough. Both rider and horse were injured by Sioux arrows. Their movement across the land was slow. Hotah took his time. He wanted to do this thing just right. But he would have to stop them before they reached the big river; before the big villages of white men. Staying out of sight had also been easy. Trees, tall grasses and plenty of hills and ravines helped him stay hidden as he traveled. As they moved further east, the number of the hills and small valleys increased.

Hotah still could not understand why his father had let a white man talk him into leading a small war party west, to the land of tall hills beyond the buffalo hunting grounds. He could not understand why his father had allowed his younger brother to join the hunting party. His brother, Enapay, had returned wrapped in animal skins and tied to a travois. Enapay was dead. Their father blamed himself. Hotah saw no reason to disagree. Yet he had let go of his anger, his hatred for these people who had killed his brother. His father and the village medicine man had convinced him to do so.

This was different, though,and the spirit signs could not be ignored.     They had thought they were safe. Well south of the area of the big fights in New Ulm and the hanging massacre in Mankato last winter, they were living out their normal rhythm of life in an out-of-the-way valley. Seldom did they see others, Indian or white.

This white man he was following and his three crazed companions had attacked Hotah and his friends for no reason. That they intended to kill and scalp them all could not be argued. In their unprovoked attack on Hotah's hunting party, this crazy white man had scalped Wicasa with a tomahawk as he rode past. The man rode his pony every bit as well as any Sioux brave Hotah had ever seen–perhaps as good as a Crow warrior.

The furious attack of the four riders caught the Sioux hunting party completely off guard. It had been so sudden there was no time to prepare; no time to defend. Wicasa was down, not moving. Hotah, Mika and Chaska had each loosed an arrow reflexively. Each arrow found a mark in one of the attacking riders. Mika loosed another arrow that slammed into the rear haunches of the crazy white man's pony. Mika's first arrow stuck like a branch from the white man's hip.

The man wheeled his pony around, now showing his short rifle in his hands. The gun barked, once, twice, a third time. Riding hard, the white man's bullets went wild. He stopped his horse to aim, but another of Mika's arrows narrowly missed his head. The rifle fired again. The rider worked the lever of the gun and took aim again. This time it was Hotah's arrow that caused the bullet to miss. The same thing happened with Chaska's arrow. The rider saw the blur and leaned forward. Both arrow and bullet flew harmlessly past their intended targets.

Mika was aiming carefully at the white devil before him. Somehow, the man jerked in his saddle and swung his upper body down while again working the lever action of his short rifle. The shot that killed Mika was actually fired alongside the horse's belly. An instant later, the white man was gone, racing into the distance. Hotah urged his pony into a fierce gallop following, then gave up a short distance later when the white man entered a thickly wooded ravine.

After turning back, he found one of the four attackers face-down with an arrow in his spine. Hotah jumped down from his pony, drew his knife, stooped and swiftly removed the man's scalp. He continued on foot back to the scene of the fighting. Mika and Wicasa were both dead. Chaska was holding his hand to his own head where one of the attackers' tomahawks had gouged him deeply in a failed attempt to remove another scalp. What was wrong with these white men? Chaska was well enough to ride back to their village after Hotah helped him bind his wound with some leaves and rawhide strips.

Hotah put the memories of the attack out of his mind. He had followed the crazy white man many miles, down the Turkey River valley, always staying out of sight. The white man should be killed while he felt safe, as Hotah and his friends had felt. The white man stopped walking at the top of the hill. The sun was setting. It was perfect. Hotah was ready to loose his arrow.

The sound of a heavy horse loping up the opposite slope from where Hotah hid caused him to relax the draw of the arrow in his bow. A moment later, a large white man on a huge horse crested the hilltop and the sound of a wagon and team reached his ears.

Until yesterday, Hotah had seen his spirit animal, a mountain lion, each day along his journey. The village medicine man often instructed him on the importance of paying attention to his spirit animal. Thus, with no appearance of the lion today and these additional white people arriving, Hotah decided to end his man-hunt...for today. Doing this thing right was more important than doing it in a hurry. Hotah would wait to see what the lion did tomorrow, or the next day.

Hotah remembered to meditate as a way of calming his own spirit during the period of waiting. He monitored his breathing and watched the other animals for their spirit guidance, and the moon for its leading. It was hard to be patient during those days of waiting, with the evil white man so close, between Hotah and the river. Or maybe he was traveling away from him on the other side. Hotah had no way of knowing.

Then finally, on the night of the full moon, he saw Imuntanka–the mountain lion, leap from a tree branch. The big cat landed on the unsuspecting rabbit, snapping its neck and killing it instantly.

His spirit animal appearing to him under the full moon was powerful medicine. Hotah considered the signs carefully. He did not want to do this thing wrong. Tomorrow night, he would drop from a high place onto his unsuspecting quarry, as his guide had showed him. He was as certain that this would happen in just this way, more certain than anything before in his life.

Instead of breaking the man's neck, he would cut it. That way, the evil man would die slowly, knowing who had killed him and why. Hotah knew that his spirit animal, his guide, approved. The tingling hair on his neck confirmed this truth.

\* \* \*

*Tuesday, October 27, 1863. At the edge of the livery barn and yard of the Hotel Julien, uphill from the hotel on Second Street.*

Their days in the Hotel Julien passed enjoyably, if too quickly. Doctor Mason declared that Wilson was fit to travel and should find a surgeon to look at his wound as soon as possible to ensure there was no spreading infection. The liverymen from the hotel's stable assured Finn and Walters that all the animals were in traveling condition, as was the wagon. Xander, Wilson's mount, was declared available to travel, with the added conditions that "it be light, easy riding, no galloping, and no more than six hours in a day." The arrow had not gone so deep, nor done as much damage to the horse's hip as was originally thought.

Finn and Walters had been busy conducting agency and personal business during their stay in the hotel. They had learned of the ferry accident at Muscatine and the loss of the wagon. Both Babcock and Thatcher were due to join them on the Dunleith side of the river the next day. Pinkerton had wired words of encouragement to the entire team, even adding therein his reflection of thanks that no one had been hurt or lost in the mishap.

Finn's telegram to Maggie received a prompt return that all was fine in Delavan. Walters' letter and wire to his sister in St. Louis received a most encouraging response: Radlyn Walters Holub, now known as Elizabeth Upchurch, would be happy to visit them all in Delavan in the coming weeks. She expressed her interest in learning more of the business opportunities that her brother and Rob Finn wanted to discuss.

In settling the charges with the hotel, Rob had already taken care of the doctor's fees. Thus there was no need of extended discussion between them. Things looked to be improving. Doctor Mason would check over Wilson's bandages and wounds in the morning before the group left from the hotel's livery stable.

After completing his exam, Mason's advice was that Wilson ride in the wagon rather than on horseback. Wilson replied that this "was the longest stretch in nearly thirty years that he had not been on a horse, and he was going to ride at least a few miles that day no matter what the doctor ordered." Nevertheless, Wilson agreed to ride in the wagon until after they were on the Illinois side of the Mississippi.

Doctor Mason shrugged at Wilson's comment; it was not the first time a patient stated their plan to not follow doctor's orders. But it was probably the first time his medical bag was without the emergency scalpel he always carried there. Mason was unaware that the instrument was missing.

Arrangements for crossing the Mississippi aboard the side-wheeled steamboat, A.F. Gregoire, were completed the day before and the fares paid. Only the final loading of their trappings remained to be done before they would ride the short distance to the wharf to embark.

Billy Adams insisted on pulling his share of the weight within the traveling company. He repeatedly climbed into the wagon's cabin carrying the baggage of others before hoisting his own valise aboard and following it into the large room on wheels. He needed to change his shirt and put on his warmest coat for today's travel. As he settled the heavy coat into place, the prick of the sharp blade point at his throat totally surprised him.

"Quiet now, boy. I don't wanna hurt you. Nobody needs to get hurt or killed. Just listen to me, and do what I tell you. Understand?" Billy recognized Wilson's voice at once.

"But ..."

"No talking, no questions!" Wilson's voice filled with menace as the blade pressed deeper against Billy's neck where it joined his shoulder. The small cut would be hidden from sight by the collar of his jacket. "Nod if you understand, make a noise and you'll die."

Billy nodded his understanding.

"Good. Keep listening. I got to leave this party and I'm taking what belongs to me with. That's no concern of yours. Finn and Walters likely have other ideas about that.

I don't want to shoot either of them, but I will if I have to. Understand?"

Billy nodded again.

"Good. I need you to ride along with me for a couple hours today. Then you'll be free to go. I need you to ride Roxie with the packages I put in her saddle bags. We'll be done by dark. I promise. Then you'll be free as the wind again. Can you do that?"

Billy did not hesitate to nod his agreement.

Wilson was quiet and calm as he finished his instructions. "You and me were both soldiers under orders, so I know you can follow mine. Here's my orders: You are going to walk out the wagon door to where Roxie is hitched right behind, then climb into her saddle. Don't look at anybody, don't say a word. I'm gonna have my carbine pointed at your head the whole time. I'll do the talking for both of us. You'll hear what I tell the others, then you and I are gonna ride away west up that hill. Only until dark, then you're free. Do just like I've told you, and everybody will be just fine. Understand?"

Billy nodded again, sure in his mind that this plan couldn't work. Rob, or Lonnie, or Patrick was certain to shoot this madman. And he took some comfort from the pocket knife he carried inside a flap in the cuff of his heavy coat. It was the same knife he had held clenched in his fist when he clobbered the drunken Reb back in Denver. With its heft and hardness, the folded Barlow turned Billy's swinging fist into a walloping club.

With Patrick's help, he had learned to remove the knife from its hiding spot, open the blade, and throw it accurately–all with one hand. True, it had been a game to help him improve his use of his left hand and arm. They'd practiced it so many times, he could do it in his sleep. Billy told himself he would be ready when the time came for whatever happened.

\* \* \*

*Tuesday, October 27, 1863. On a game trail about seven miles northwest of Dubuque, Iowa. Late evening with the full moon nearly overhead.*

Things at the hotel livery yard had gone almost exactly the way John Wilson laid them out in his explanation to Billy. Rob and the others stood transfixed while Wilson held his cocked Spencer carbine aimed at Billy's head and explained his plan of escape. Rob, Lonnie, and Patrick kept their distance while Wilson lead Billy out of town on horseback. Lonnie and Patrick stayed behind to watch over the wagon and team; Rob followed on Bricks about a quarter-mile behind. Finn hoped for an opportunity to rescue Billy. He didn't know what it might look like when it happened, but he was alert for any opening.

\* \* \*

*Tuesday, October 17, 1863. After dark, with the full moon high above the trail leading northwest above the Turkey River.*

Billy Adams' fears decreased as the day wore on. Nothing happened to upset their passage through the Turkey River valley. Wilson had shared some of his jerky and hardtack and had been conversational at times as they rode along. More than once he reminded Billy that, if Billy gave him no trouble, he would soon be free. At times Billy could see Rob Finn in the distance behind them. Once, when Wilson caught him turned in his saddle looking backward, the man remarked, "Don't worry, son. Finn ain't gonna do anything to set you free before I'm ready to send you on your way. You'll see soon enough."

There had been a light snow up here above the Mississipi. Billy noticed paw prints in the late afternoon that appeared to have been made by a giant cat. Since the sun dropped below the horizon, he wondered if and when Wilson would finally set him free, in keeping with his word.

Almost as if he read Billy's mind, Wilson reigned his horse in and turned them both around as they entered under the oak tree's canopy. The tree had lost most of its leaves, but enough remained to put them into shadow, hidden from the bright moon-glow of the cloudless night.

Wilson put a cupped hand to his mouth and called out in a loud voice, "Finn! I am lettin' Billy go right here. Sending him back to you. Do not try any fancy shootin' with that Sharps, and everything will be fine. And do not try followin' me. I know how to watch and cover my back trail. Understand me?" Wilson had called slowly and deliberately. There was no echo.

Several moments later, they heard Rob's slow, clear answer, " I understand, Wilson. If Billy's unhurt, I will not follow you."

Wilson still had the rifle aimed at Billy. He said, "Steady that horse now, just one more thing to do." He had dismounted and walked to Billy's side as he spoke. "Now open up them saddle bags and sit real still while I retrieve what rightfully belongs to me."

Billy knew that this would be his chance to prove himself to his friends. He worked the clasp-knife down his wrist and into his hand. He worked furiously to open the blade, thinking he would stab Wilson in the eye and call for Rob's help. His heart lurched into his throat when the knife hit the ground behind Roxie's left front hoof.

Wilson jumped at the noise, then moved to see what had caused it. Billy hadn't yet opened the blade, so no glint of steel helped give away the knife's location. As Wilson bent to examine the ground with his hand, the dark shadow of a huge cat blurred past Billy, landing on the stooped-over man. A loud snarl was followed by a shriek cut short. There was another snarl.

Roxie didn't budge during the action going on literally under her feet. A pair of gleaming eyes transfixed young Adams in his saddle, then they were gone. The huge cat covered the ground between the shadow of the tree and a nearby ravine at incredible speed. Billy thought his eyes played tricks on him when the big cat reared up on its hind legs before going over the edge. He was too shaken to follow.

By the time Finn reached him, Wilson realized he wouldn't be greeting the morning sun. He was quick to offer his apology for the trouble he had caused and for lives lost. His breathing was labored; the lacerations across his neck allowing his life's blood to escape. Following his brief apology, Wilson spoke quickly while he yet could, "How long have you known, Rob?"

Rob answered truthfully, "It seemed mighty odd you walking right up t' the crest of that ridge above Bannack last July. Seemed even stranger–you not bein' sure it was Emry down below, but bein' able t' identify the Sioux at that distance. Been watchin' you real close since then. The ambush on Grasshopper Creek the night we left Bannack, that was the sure giveaway. Save your breath, Wilson. I'm not lookin' for any answers from ya now."

Wilson nodded his head. A look of deep shame and sorrow filled his eyes. "I wouldn't have hurt this boy, Rob ... ya' got t' ..." Wilson's words trailed off as life left his body.

"I'm sure you didn't mean to hurt anyone, Wilson," Rob said. "Things just got out of hand, the way they always do on that path." Finn knew Wilson was dead. His words were intended for his own and Billy's benefit.

# CHAPTER NINE

# The Circuses Come To Town

*Late October 1863. Bannack, Idaho Territory.*

During the weeks that the wagon party spent in Denver and those weeks after they left Denver, (journeying across Colorado and Nebraska Territories and the State of Iowa), the rest of the country was in a flurry of activity. The Mabie Menagerie and Circus was busy working the crowds in Minnesota and Iowa. Meanwhile folks living in, arriving in, or leaving from Bannack and Virginia City mining districts had not been idle. Virginia City grew rapidly; Bannack continued to produce gold even though some miners had left for the greener pastures of Alder Gulch.

Back in the States, the War Between the States continued with skirmishes across the southern and the eastern theaters of the conflict. State and Federal government troops continued to harass Indian tribes out of their ancestral regions of habitation according to the Indian Removal Act of 1830. Removal activities were especially aggressive in the states of Minnesota and Iowa , and in the Dakota Territory.

Members of the Mormon religion, having earlier been chased west and east across Missouri and Iowa, were still seeking to practice their beliefs without interference from governments. Since settling in Salt Lake City, they were continuing their plans for the State of Deseret. The Lincoln Administration was determined that they should not have it, but Lincoln himself was exercising every caution to avoid provoking the growing church and its ambitious leader, Brigham Young. Real peace was nowhere to be found on the continent.

Electa Plummer had ridden the stagecoach to Salt Lake City as her husband, Henry, rode on horseback alongside. At the ferry crossing outside Idaho Falls, the Sidney Edgerton family needed to move aside to allow for the stage coach and its accompanying outrider, Sheriff Henry Plummer, to disembark. The Edgerton party, including son-in-law Wilbur Sanders, were anxious to cross the river and complete their trip. They had been hoping to travel as far west as Lewiston, Idaho Territory before winter set in, but recent drops in temperature suggested they might very well be wintering-over in Bannack.

When saying their parting good-byes in Salt Lake City, Electa asked her husband again for his promise to leave Bannack as soon as possible and join her in Cedar Rapids, Iowa. Henry agreed and reminded his wife to look out for her own safety, saying that, "Not all who seem peaceable can be trusted, even in government positions."

Electa nodded her agreement with her husband's advice. It was an emotional parting for them both.

Sidney Edgerton's family had arrived in Bannack on September 18th. They were not favorably impressed with the sights, sounds, and smells that greeted them. The first alarming news they received after their arrival was of the robbery and murder of Lloyd Magruder in mid-October.

Another robbery occurred about ten days later, when the Peabody and Caldwell coach was robbed on October 23rd. A mere three weeks later, a teenager that the families hired to round up some horses was held at gun point, or so he told Edgerton. Young Henry Tilden further informed his employers that one of the robbers was Sheriff Plummer. Edgerton and Sanders believed the youngster's story without checking any evidence and with no other witnesses. Nine days later, a stagecoach belonging to the A.J. Oliver Express service was robbed at gunpoint. To the Edgerton-Sanders family members, Bannack seemed the most violent city on Earth.

* * *

*Sunday, November 1, 1863. On the road east of Galena, Illinois.*

The hastily convened coroner's inquest in Dubuque had accepted Rob's and Billy's testimonies regarding Wilson's death. They ruled the man had been killed by a wild animal, probably the same mountain lion that had been reported in the vicinity during recent weeks. Nearby paw prints found in the fresh snow lent credence to their conclusion. The inquiry process delayed the Finn party's departure from the city, but only by three additional days. The travelers settled back into their routine of luxury-hotel living without complaint.

Crossing the Mississippi into Dunleith finally took place on Saturday, and they hurried into Galena, urged on by what appeared to be another incoming storm. They continued on once the threat of weather passed them by, eager to make up for time lost during the Wilson incident.

Reading a day-old copy of the Freeport Daily Journal picked up as they left Galena, Illinois, Rob Finn became concerned at the attention being paid his young son. His parental instinct was responding to the knowledge of how easy it would be for the youngster to have his head turned. John was pictured with trainer Stewart Craven on the front page of the paper. Underneath the photograph was the announcement of the circus's arrival in Freeport this week, where it would open for business east of town on the road to Rockford, Illinois. The circus intended to stay for up to one week before packing up for a show in Beloit, Wisconsin on its way to winter quarters in Delavan. Despite Rob's fatherly concern that his son get a swelled head from all the attention, he was quite proud of the lad.

Lonnie drove the mule team of their converted circus wagon. Finn estimated they might need only another full day's travel to reach Freeport, assuming the weather did not turn against them. Finn turned to Walters and asked, "I wonder, can we make Freeport by tomorrow night?"

Taking the hint that his friend would like to make that arrival more certain, Walters snapped the traces gently calling out the encouragement, "High on." He then faced Rob to say, "I think we'll be there in plenty of time, Rob. This team don't seem to mind these hills 'n' valleys even a little bit, and that's the truth." He smiled.

∗ ∗ ∗

*Monday, November 2, 1863. The Mabie Circus riding on the Illinois Central Railroad Line between Dixon, Illinois and Freeport, Illinois.*

Some days, it was the cost of the railway transportation that decided which towns the circus visited. Usually it was the size of the population and the circus operator's perception of how anxious a particular community might be to pay the price of admission. Sometimes other factors entered into the mix for deciding where to go, how long to play a town, when to leave. The weather was not to be overlooked either, especially from harvest time and later in the year.

This year, the Mabie Brothers Circus of Delavan, Wisconsin had been doing exceptionally well. People were eager for entertainment to take their minds off the terrible war ripping the nation apart. Mabie's Grand Menagerie was how the circus was being billed to emphasize their animal attractions. Other attractions included performers who did complex and dangerous feats high above the crowds or on horseback. The circus also had a sideshow of oddities for additional drawing power.

Then the incident with Romeo in Minneapolis occurred and the emergence of a young hero caught the attention of the newspapers. Following that, every town down the line of the Burlington, Cedar Rapids, and Minnesota Railway wanted the circus to pay them a visit. Some promised or even guaranteed worthwhile gate receipts for the traveling troupe.

As a result, the traveling show played to full audiences in Mankato and Albert Lea before crossing into Iowa. They performed in front of thronging crowds in Cedar Falls, Waterloo, Cedar Rapids, and Iowa City. They played for three days on both sides of the river: in Davenport, Iowa and just outside Moline. The packed grandstands for every show were testimony to the citizens' desire for the curiosities presented. Sideshow oddities, tumbling exhibitions, and enactments of Indian bands were all as popular as the animal and high-wire shows. Edmund Mabie was making money hand-over-fist.

The Mabie brothers were good businessmen. They were known to be fair with their employees, if somewhat tight-fisted with their money. Edmund Mabie also knew that there were times when a little extra generosity could pay big dividends. He had already decided to make a special gift to John Finn as a gesture of appreciation for his heroism in the training cage. Edmund did not yet know what that gift would be, but he planned to present it during a special ceremony, probably after they returned to Delavan.

Reporters in each town having a newspaper interviewed famed elephant trainer Stewart Craven. They also interviewed John Finn, the boy hero credited with saving Craven from Romeo's raging charge. John was becoming impressed with his growing celebrity over the incident. The crowds in Mendota and Dixon, Illinois had been even more enthusiastic and welcoming than those in Iowa towns. It seemed John's fame was growing as the circus neared home.

* * *

*Tuesday, November 3, 1863. Freeport, Illinois. The Brewster House Hotel.*

Though it would pale in comparison to The Hotel Julien they had so lately quit in Dubuque, the Brewster House in Freeport was a very nice accommodation for people who often slept out-of-doors, or in wagons, or in rooms without heat. The Brewster House boasted comfortable beds, heated rooms, heated baths, excellent menu fare at reasonable prices, fresh ice-cream treats for dessert. All of which were appreciated by each of the four members yet heading for Delavan. Rob appreciated the lower prices since he was picking up the tab for all of the others.

None of this group of hotel guests even noticed that both Senator Stephen Douglas and his debate opponent had stayed in this building during the 1858 debates. Billy and Patrick did not know of those famous debates nor the two contestants. Both had been too young at that time to care about such things. Rob wondered if the current President would yet recall such a homey and humble place as The Brewster House in Freeport with the same fondness that he himself felt toward the providers of hospitality to travelers.

Or perhaps Abraham Lincoln never had thoughts of events five years earlier. He was understandably quite occupied with the war and the running of the country.

* * *

*Wednesday, November 4, 1863. The road east from the Illinois Central Railway siding in Freeport, Illinois.*

Getting the maximum publicity from unusual things or events was the bailiwick of politicians and entertainers. Edmund Mabie fully understood the importance of gaining public recognition for his circuses to promote gate receipts.

To that end he had recently changed procedures for entering the towns where they would perform.

As usual, the railroad cars carrying the circus wagons, acts, animals and equipment would be pulled to a siding, and a parade through the town arranged. The new twist since leaving Minneapolis was to have young John Finn, hero of the training cage, ride Juliet at the head of the parade. The crowds did not know that Juliet was the smaller, docile female of the circus menagerie's two elephants. They assumed the lad to be riding the famed "killer elephant", Romeo. Truth was that Romeo was never allowed in parades and spent most of his time in a large cage, hidden inside a tent.

John was decked out in a splendid uniform, complete with tasseled hat, fancy vest and boots. He even had a decorated whip in his hand. Though John was under strict orders from Stewart Craven never to use the whip, people in the crowd were awed to think the young man controlled mighty elephants with the small, colorful device. Thus convinced, the crowds followed the parade to where the show was being set up for their enjoyment, usually on a fairgrounds or in a large field on the outside edge of town.

As he spotted his son riding atop the elephant, leading the entire circus parade from the siding where the rail cars carrying them were parked, Rob felt a swell of pride in how the boy carried himself. John waved and smiled at the crowd as genuinely as if they had been his own friends or neighbors back in Delavan. He ignored personal jibes yelled by trouble-makers in the crowd–all crowds have hecklers, and John already had the wisdom and experience not to show them any notice. That the elephant was well-trained and obedient was obvious, but Rob could not help but notice that his not-quite eleven-year-old boy behaved maturely and professionally. What father wouldn't be proud of a son like that?

And yet, that very observation added to Rob's personal dilemma: should he call out and try to get John's attention? He had no desire to distract nor embarrass this son. The first could be dangerous, the second impolite. Both were possible outcomes if he should succeed in gaining his son's notice. A short moment later that option was past, along with the parade heading to the circus grounds east of the city. Since the moment was lost, John would receive his father's handwritten note whenever the messenger caught up with him, and that would have to be good enough.

Rob sighed at the realization that he would not see his son John face-to-face until the circus arrived in Delavan. Perhaps that was for the best.

\* \* \*

*Thrusday, November 26, 1863, Thanksgiving Day.*
*Bannack, Idaho Territory.*

Chief Justice Edgerton chose not to announce his documented authority and appointment by the President of the US at this time. He told his family that he saw little point in frustrating the law or himself by trying to establish a bench of justice in such an environment of brigands, ruffians, and criminal types. He would establish his bench of territorial justice next spring, when they finally reached Lewiston. As things developed, Edgerton never did reach Lewiston the next spring, or at all.

It must have seemed a bright beacon of hope to these beleaguered midwesterners that the Thanksgiving feast took place a mere four days after the latest robbery. The host was none other than Sheriff Henry Plummer, he having invited them to attend his offered celebration shortly after they arrived in town. Since this was the first National Thanksgiving Day celebration ever held, (having been decreed by presidential order the previous month), no one knew quite what to expect.

Henry Plummer spared no expense preparing for this Thanksgiving dinner. In addition to a wide display of fine wines, delicate pastries and breads, and sumptuous offerings of relishes, his table centerpiece was a large roasted turkey, brought in at considerable cost from Salt Lake City. Even more beautiful than the golden brown skin of the bird was the wonderful aroma wafting from the tray. Guests that evening would comment favorably about this meal for years to come; even the finicky Mrs. Edgerton and Mrs. Sanders proclaimed it to have been an excellent dining experience.

In addition to the exquisite table laid before his guests by their host, Henry Plummer's mannerisms and speech charmed them all. The ladies, both young and old, responded to his respectful attention with blushes on their faces. They were surprised when Plummer asked their opinions, and then even more surprised when he listened to their responses. Sidney Edgerton and his son-in-law Wilbur Sanders both began to harbor doubts about their own earlier assessments of Plummer, at one point exchanging a puzzled look between them. Had they judged and acted in haste, they wondered? Could such a smooth, likable dinner companion and host be a blood-thirsty outlaw?

During a private conversation together two days later, Edgerton remarked to Sanders that "time would tell" the truth about Henry Plummer. It sounded like sage advice–counseling patience in matters of justice dealing with the locally-elected sheriff.

# CHAPTER TEN

# Home At Last

*Thursday, November 26, 1863 Thanksgiving Day. The Finn family farm in Delavan, Wisconsin. Thursday, November 26, 1863 Thanksgiving Day. The Finn family farm in Delavan, Wisconsin.*

For three decades people had been singing "be it ever so humble, there's no place like home". The phrase recurred to Rob frequently since returning to the comforts of home and hearth the first week of the month. He was pleased with the way his son, John, responded to his father's thoughts about circus life, humility, celebrity, and obedience. John and Maggie had been getting along well in the wake of their family discussions on those matters.

Patrick had taken to the farm and the town as though born there. He had a quick smile for everyone, and went out of his way to help Maggie around the house. In his spare time, Patrick was helping Lonnie lay out a new barn and paddock for the eventual horse-breeding and training business that Walters planned to start in the spring. The house being built for Radlyn Walters and Lonnie was being done by a professional building firm from Lake Geneva, and was coming along well.

Lonnie had been successful in finding a horse breeder in Spring Grove, Illinois who had an excellent line to select from and was willing to work with him to develop additional superior lines.

Even young Billy Adams, who had been certain his family would reject him due to his missing limb, had landed well. His family received him lovingly, and his mother and father did not even chastise him for thinking there was any chance they wouldn't welcome him home. His friend Patrick Murphy stopped in at the Adams family farm in Walworth at least twice a week. It was becoming less sure whether he was there to visit his friend Billy, or Billy's pretty sister, Jenna. It didn't really matter. The whole family enjoyed Patrick's warm manner. They also appreciated how much Patrick had helped their Billy make adjustments to his new life.

With little more to think about for the rest of the day than carving, serving, and enjoying turkey for the family's first-ever Thanksgiving dinner, Rob was relaxing before the fireplace in the parlor. Lonnie, Patrick, Billy and John were likewise enjoying the warmth and leisurely camraderie of the comfortable room.

Lonnie's sister Radlyn was helping in the kitchen at her own insistence. Lonnie was privately certain those joining at the table would soon agree that his sister was an excellent cook. In addition to her business acumen as an investment advisor, the woman loved to cook and entertain, and was accomplished at both. Once her home was built here on the farm property, she planned on doing a fair amount of both. She wanted her new neighbors to get to know her and hoped to get to know them, as well. That might have to wait until next spring, but she could be patient. It was a trait she had learned the hard way.

Radlyn Walters Holub learned of her widowhood a few months earlier. Years before, she had escaped the controlling clutches of her husband, Curtiss Holub, who had become abusive toward her during his frequent bouts of drunkenness. She left behind the beautiful Kentucky bluegrass region of her youth, moving to St. Louis, Missouri to begin her new life as Elizabeth Upchurch. She lived and operated her investment business in St. Louis during those years after leaving Kentucky.

Since learning of her husband Curtiss' death, and now that she was moving to Delavan, Wisconsin to be near her brother Lonnie, she resumed use of her given, unmarried name. It gave her great joy to again be called Radlyn Walters, as though a burden had been removed.

As for her estranged husband's death, Radlyn could not help wondering if it really was accidental. Drowning in one's own bathwater was not unheard of, and Curtiss certainly drank enough alcohol to account for such an event. Yet it was possible that one or more of the many people who had grown to hate the man had a hand in his death. Curtiss had grown more dislikable and abusive during the years she was with him. He may have continued his bad behaviors in the years since she left. Anything was possible.

No matter how he died, Radlyn felt no sorrow when she learned of his passing–only relief that she was finally free from the worry of Curtiss Holub ever finding her or causing her more trouble or pain. The fortune she had accumulated had always been her own; now there could be no contest of her rights to her own money using the laws of those states wherein the husband held all claim to marital property.

Thus, when her brother Lonnie's letters and telegrams inviting her participation in a business investment venture and to relocate her residence to Delavan, Wisconsin arrived this September past, she had nothing to stop her. And she wanted very much to again be with her brother. Radlyn had no children of her own and was beyond childbearing age. She wanted no husband. Lonnie wanted no wife. The two of them could live well together as brother and sister, caring for one another and sharing a house and their material wealth. It would be a wonderful way to spend their remaining years of life.

Radlyn's investment talents would be put to use managing the funds of her brother, and the Finn family, and the private wealth of the Odgen trove. The proceeds from investing the Ogden trove would be donated anonymously each year to several select charities, including the Wisconsin School for the Deaf in Delavan. Other institutions serving the needs of children and especially Indian children would also benefit from this trust fund.

There was also the special, and very secret, fund established to return stolen gold to those miners and shippers victimized by Wilson and Emry. Five living people knew of this money and its source: Rob, Lonnie, Pinkerton, Babcock, and Radlyn.

Gold in this fund was that which had been presumed lost when the barge went down during the crossing at Muscatine. What had actually been on that wagon was a load of lead ore that had been swapped out at Pinkerton's suggestion.

Returning this gold to its rightful owners was an involved process because Radlyn, Lonnie, and Rob exercised infinite care in tracking down, investigating, and returning money to claimants. The process started with placing blind advertisements in newspapers around the country. They knew it would take many years to find all who had been robbed, and they set about the work with energy and determination.

Then there was the income from their claim in Bannack. Ned McNally was given a one-half ownership interest in the claim to continue working it. The man was as honest as they could wish for, in addition to being hard-working. Their claim produced high-grade gold dust and nuggets each week and Ned reported and deposited it all faithfully. Radlyn would be investing this money as it came in, along with the rest of the funds she was tending.

Income produced by this source would augment that from the other enterprises of the Walters and Finns.

Two other happy circumstances arose from these arrangements. Radlyn would be able to start her investment-advising business in Delavan for customers there, while continuing to handle many of her customers from St. Louis via telegraph and mail. Telegraph lines and railroads were changing the world rapidly and those who adjusted quickly and well would thrive and prosper.

To handle the workload, Radlyn would need to hire a clerk. After a three-hour-long interview, she and the woman being screened decided it would be a good fit. Catherine Finn Duffy would come to work for Radlyn Walters in the spring of 1864, once the new house was ready. Catherine would happily have her son, Thomas Duffy, III, with her. Rob, John, and Mary were excited for the anticipated reuniting; Robert Finn, Jr., at age four, was too young to understand having his sister and nephew living close.

Not everything could turn out as hoped for. In November, Catherine had nearly changed her position regarding Maggie in order to accept Rob's invitation to the family Thanksgiving dinner. However, since Maggie continued refusing to apologize for her harsh remarks of the year before, Catherine declined the invitation. Once again her father was furious with his new wife's stubbornness.

Allan Pinkerton had been aware of switching loads before the wagons left Denver. In fact, he had been the architect of the plan. Pinkerton was actively involved in the New York City and Washington, D.C. government and banking sectors. So much so that he was more often frustrated and sickened by what he saw being done with public funds. Knowing Finn and Walters to be honest men, Pinkerton believed the best chance for the stolen money being returned to its rightful owners lay in Rob's and Lonnie's faithful hands–not in the hands of government employees or bankers.

Thus it was Pinkerton who ordered crates of lead ore (of the same dimensions as the boxes of gold coins) be swapped for the crated load of coined, stolen Bannack gold. He further authorized that shipment be sent to his agency offices in Chicago, planning to come up with another explanation when the switch was "discovered." The ferrying accident at Muscatine was an unplanned bonus. There would be no way to recover those crates intact from the Mississippi River. The river would take care of hiding the evidence as it tumbled the lead ore downstream amid the silt and mud. Pinkerton would not have planned things to go the way they did because of the inherent danger to the men involved. He thanked Providence for the intervention, however.

Babcock had known of the switch and that the sturdy green circus wagon was carrying a double shipment of gold. Thatcher was never told, nor was Caleb Agnew, the young soldier escort who found his own courage that day. Babcock was already back in Washington, D. C., or on another assignment. Asa Thatcher had developed a cough that lasted long enough to get him medically assigned to recuperate at his parents' farm, making his mother an especially happy woman. During his recovery, and at Rob's instigation, the Pinkerton Agency was quietly working to recruit Thatcher away from the BMI.

Maggie Finn was feeling the physical strain of her pregnancy. Her back, legs, and feet hurt. She was exhausted by tasks that, under normal circumstances, would not affect her in the least. It was difficult to bend over and she was uncomfortable most of the time. In the seventh month of pregnancy, these things contributed to her shortness of breath and her shortness of temper. Add to this a house filled with her returned husband, his friend Lonnie, and her step-son John–the poor woman was at wit's end. Thank God for this whirlwind helper in the kitchen, Radlyn Walters!

At Radlyn's urging, Maggie was sitting in a chair by the outside door of the kitchen. The wood-burning cookstove kept that whole end of the house warm when a big meal was being served. The door was open just a crack to allow the excess heat to escape. Maggie heard horse hooves clopping up to the front of the house as they passed by the kitchen wing. She looked up in time to miss seeing the rider, but clearly saw a fine-looking chestnut hindquarter as it continued on its way.

The knock at the front door was loud and insistent. Rob was half-way to the door when John shot past him to reach it first. John opened the door to none other than one of the brothers owning the circus, Edmund Mabie. The man was dressed in a fancy ringmaster's suit, complete with ruffle-fronted shirt, ruffled sleeve cuffs, and a top hat.

Mabie removed the top hat to say, "I apologize if my timing is inconvenient, but decided that this Thanksgiving Day might be the best time to favor young John with a small reward–a token of our appreciation for him saving the day for us all in Minneapolis. Do I have your permission, sir?" The question was directed to Rob.

Rob's brow arched in question, but before he could ask anything, Mabie continued, "If you disapprove, sir, I'll understand. It just seemed with you home again, and all this land ... I thought this a useful, suitable gift for a young man so good with animals." As he finished his sentence he pivoted his stance on the front porch to turn and point at the horse he had ridden up on. "She's a beauty, gentle as can be, four years old and already well-trained. Comes with all the tack and saddle, just as you see her. What d'ya say, Mr. Finn? Do you approve?"

The man was a natural salesman, and even had Rob wanted to decline the gift to his son, he knew he would have yielded in the face of such persuasive speech. And since he had no desire to not accept the horse, he readily agreed. The mare was a good gift and would be good for John.

"Certainly, Mr. Mabie! I won't deny your generosity, nor your gift to John. And I thank you most sincerely for it! Won't you step inside and join us?" It was now Rob's turn to be sincere and cordial to the guest standing in the chill of the southern Wisconsin November.

"Thank you kindly for the offer, Mr. Finn. But I must be off. Always more errands to run for our people. Perhaps another time?" Mabie winked around his big smile, then turned to watch John, who ran out past the two men upon hearing his father's acceptance of the horse.

Finn and Mabie strolled casually out to where the horse was hitched and John was already fussing over her. "She's called Sadie, but you could change that if it doesn't suit," Mabie told John. "Keep in mind we'll always have a place for you with our troupe, John, but only with your parents' permission!"

"Yes, sir, Mr. Mabie, sir. Thank you, sir. She's a fine animal, sir. I'll take good care of her always! Thank you!" John's enthusiasm was genuine and contagious. The two men laughed, then shook hands before Mabie turned to leave.

"And thank you, Mr. Finn. That's one fine boy ... er ... should I say "young man" you've raised there, one we wouldn't mind having as a regular member of our circus. No need to answer this moment, but please do think about the offer. I mean it sincerely."

Edmund Mabie paused, considered something for a moment before asking, "By the way, I don't suppose you'd be interested in selling that green wagon parked alongside your barn? We are always in need of sturdy wagons for our people. Yours seems as if it was made for circus use."

Rob chuckled his answer, "And so it was, Mr. Mabie. So it was. We bought it from a Mr. Ford in Denver who acquired it in Chicago some years back. It may be for sale. Ah hadn't thought about it. Ah'll need to ask my partner, an' it would need t' be cleaned out an' mended before we could let it go, assuming Lonnie is agreeable." To himself Rob knew they would need to remove the false floor from inside the wagon. It was that floor under which two layers of stacked cases containing gold coins rode in secret across the country.

"Well, if you do decide to let it go, all I ask is that you give me first crack at buying it." Mabie smiled and flicked his hand toward Rob in a cursory farewell wave. Then he did turn and strut away in the direction of his circus' grounds. The man walked with a purpose, wasting no time covering the frozen ground with its light patches of snow covering.

Mabie was well away from the Finn house by the time John was happily aboard Sadie. They took their first few steps together slowly; neither horse nor rider yet familiar with the other. Rob was keeping a careful eye on his mounted son, so didn't notice the buggy arriving up the road from the train station. In the buggy was none other than Allan Pinkerton, driving himself in the elegant leather covered vehicle drawn by a single horse.

Pinkerton pulled up, halted the rig, and had the horse hitched to the post within moments of alighting from the buggy. He looked and moved spryly and wore a smile. Unusual for Allan Pinkerton.

"Hope I'm not keepin' ya from yer dinner, Longshot?" He asked. As was customary for Pinkerton, he was alone. His wife Joan seldom accompanied him outside Chicago, and rarely enough within the city. Finn had received Pinkerton's acceptance telegram just three days earlier, which stated:

**Will attend.**

Typical of the Scot's manner, he wasted neither money nor words.

"Yer timing could not be better, Mr. Pinkerton." Turning to address his son, Rob called out, "John. Put Sadie in the barn with plenty of water an' hay. Give her a quick brushin' if ya like. Then get back into the house, quick-like, if ya please. You wouldn't want t' miss the fine dinner." Done with what needed to be said to his son, Rob devoted his full attention to his guest.

"Rob, after all this time, I really must insist you call me Allan." Pinkerton smiled again at his tall friend and former employee.

"Allan it is then. Would you care t' join me in the house for some refreshment, Allan?" Rob was pleased when Pinkerton accepted his invitation and they stepped inside.

After greetings were exchanged between the others present and the newcomer, Finn, Walters and Pinkerton adjourned to Rob's office to discuss a few matters privately there. Rob assured the others of the necessity of the sequestering and promised it would be as brief as possible.

While removed from the earshot of those in the sitting room, kitchen, and remainder of the house, the three detectives discussed a number of matters in rapid succession. Rob told of the news from Henry Plummer. Contained in Plummer's hand-written letter (more of a scrawl, since the disablement of Plummer's right hand) were details of the September arrival of Sidney Edgerton and his son-in-law, Wilbur Sanders, both of whom Plummer characterized as "opportunistic politicians".

Plummer's letter went on to mention the early November arrival of Captain Nick Wall and the budding friendship between all these late arrivals with Nathan Langford, Masonic organizer, former banker, and ambitious politician. Finn and Walters already knew Langford; neither held him in high regard.

Finally, Plummer's letter reported recent incidents of theft and violence, that he was determined to find and prosecute the guilty parties, and that he remained confident of "wrapping it all up" before the year was over. He then reiterated his intention of resigning as sheriff and joining his wife in Cedar Rapids, Iowa.

The letter was dated at Virginia City, Idaho Territory, November 15, 1863. It struck the readers as curious that Plummer did not post the letter from Bannack. The letter arrived in Delavan the day before, on November 25th, by express mail, which must have cost Henry a bundle.

\* \* \*

*Saturday, November 28, 1863. Delavan, Wisconsin, shortly after lunch consisting of turkey and other left-overs. Inside the large barn of the Finn family farm.*

Lonnie not only thought that selling the wagon was a good idea, he explained why doing so soon would be better than waiting. "Once that wagon is gone from this farm, Rob, people won't have any reason to think about it anymore. Nobody will be tempted to speculate why we needed such a big, sturdy wagon just to get home from out West. We could sell the mules, too. They're a good team, but we don't need 'em for anything on the farm, unless you've got other plans."

"No, Lonnie. You're right. I've no other plans for the wagon nor the mules, an' the sooner we're rid of 'em from the farm, the sooner everyone will forget we ever had 'em. Which is for the best." Rob's voice drifted off with his thoughts. He carried his handful of tools to the back end of the wagon and set them on the step leading into the entry door.

Patrick, Billy, and John rounded through the open barn door near to where the wagon was parked inside.

Rob continued, "Good that you're here just now, lads. We're about t' get started on this little project, an' there's a few things you need t' know about what we've done, an what we're goin' t' do. Lonnie?"

As was pre-arranged, Lonnie removed a folded sheet of paper from his inside coat pocket, motioning for the young men to gather for a closer look. When it was opened out completely, they could see that it was poster with a picture of young man displayed upon it. The poster said:

**Wanted**
**Dead or Alive**
**for Robbery and Murder**
(Picture)
**Cole Younger**
**Reward = $2,000.00**

Patrick gasped, "That's him! That's Cole! That's the man we met in Lawrence! He wouldn't murder anyone!"

"We're not sayin' that he did or didn't, Patrick. But it's plain the government in Missouri thinks he's guilty. If someone puts a bullet in him t' claim the reward, Younger won't have a chance t' tell his side of the story. Do you see my point, lads?" As Rob asked his question he looked around him at the young faces that were staring at the poster. Patrick and Billy both were flushed with emotion and excitement. Both expressed surprise and shook their heads in disbelief. They didn't want to believe what the poster announced.

Rob turned his attention to the poster, at which he pointed, and said to his audience, "And let this be the lesson t' you: Whether it is true or not, what gets printed on a poster or in a newspaper is what people will believe. They shouldn't; they should question everything. But few people will question what they're told. Be among those few, lads. Question everything until you are convinced you have the truth of the matter."

Knowing his message would sink in with Patrick and Billy because of their emotional attachment to the accused, Rob wanted to draw John into the lesson as well. "That's a good path for all of us t' follow, John, though it's harder t' do when you're young. Do you understand what I'm sayin'?"

John nodded that he understood. His wide, intelligent eyes told his father that the idea had landed in the boy's brain.

It was Lonnie's turn to add a measure of wisdom to the moment. Speaking to Patrick and Billy, he said, "We listened in Denver when you told us of your run-in with Younger and the others. It was obvious you liked him and trusted him. He might be the man you think his is; he might not. The law is after him, and a reward like this is serious business. Some men will hunt him for the money, and they won't hesitate to shoot him on sight. Mr. Younger is in deep trouble, whether he deserves it or not."

Rob didn't want to dwell overlong on the shocking news he and Lonnie had presented. There was more to show and more to tell. He walked to the rear of the wagon and opened the entry door for all to see inside. It was broad daylight and the open barn door allowed for the light to wash into the compartment.

Again signaling for his audience to get nearer, Rob leaned into the back of the big compartment and easily removed two floorboards with the help of a small pry bar. Moving out of the way himself, he then invited his interested spectators to step up and investigate for themselves the opening thus revealed.

Ever since the episode with John Walters took place, Billy had been certain that some such compartment must be hidden somewhere in the spacious wagon. The space between the floors was large enough for two layers of the shallow coin crates to be hidden. And it ran the length and width of the entire wagon bed.

Patrick privately wondered how many of the small crates they had carried across the country. He then thought about the wagon lost at Muscatine and the wagon Jenks drove to St. Louis. Though he had no accurate notion of the dollar value of the cargo they had hauled, the realization hit him that the total amount must have been stunning. He showed maturity and wisdom by not mentioning his thoughts aloud.

Following these revelations, Rob summarized the points he wanted the three young men to absorb. First he spoke about John Wilson. "Ah don't say that John was a bad man, nor that he was a good one. John did some good things in his life an' behaved as a friend toward me on several occasions. He had some bad luck early on in life, an' did his best t' make his own way in the world. A lot of people liked John an' benefitted from his services. The plain fact is, once a man steps off the path of good choices onto the other path, he can slip an' slide downward mighty fast. Ah think that's what happened to John Wilson. He just wanted a little for himself an' decided t' take it. Then the little turned into a lot, an' that turned into greed ... the kind of greed that destroys a man an' those around him.

"Ah believe John Wilson never meant t' do some of the things he did. He liked people an' was neighborly t' his Indian friends an' his customers in Bannack an' Salt Lake City. He got caught up in something that is more powerful than he was, more powerful than any man. Ah'll say it again: Don't let greed become your master–not a tiny bit of it!

"Ah thought of John Wilson as a friend, but in the end, he wasn't one. Our friend in Bannack, Henry Plummer, is doing his level best t' clean up a mess caused by John Wilson an' Timothy Emry. Now it seems a few more government types have arrived out there t' muddy the waters even more. An' we'll have our hands full here tryin' t' sort out some of that same mess. It'll take months if not years, t' figure it all out. Some of those newcomers t' Bannack are in a big hurry t' solve it all real quick-like.

"Patrick an' Billy believe Cole Younger t' be a decent man, an' though he may be, the law disagrees. This wagon looks like it is meant only t' travel an' sleep in, when in fact it can carry a hidden fortune. What I'm hoping you lads will remember is this: People aren't always what they make themselves out t' be. Things are not always what they appear t' be. Pay attention an' question everything. Life goes fast–ya don't want t' miss it!"

Rob smiled his big warm Irish smile, turned to his friend Lonnie and nodded. Lonnie smiled and nodded back at the big Irishman. The lesson was over. For now. The two former Pinkerton detectives finished removing the false floor and other modifications from the wagon in preparation for delivering it to the Mabie Brothers the following week.

\* \* \*

*Christmas Week, December 1863. Bannack and Virginia City Mining Districts, Idaho Territory.*

Following three separate episodes of robbery at gunpoint in early-to-mid December, a miners' court was convened at which Wilbur Sanders prosecuted George Ives in Virginia City for the murder of young Nicholas Tiebolt. The three-day extravaganza found Ives guilty of the charge, despite questionable court procedure, and Ives was hanged on December 21st.

Two days later, the Vigilance Committee formed itself from "leading citizens" of Virginia City and Bannack. No one seemed to notice that, of those leading citizens forming the committee, several of them had arrived in the district less than sixty days prior, including Wilbur Sanders, Nick Wall, and Sidney Edgerton. The mob's blood was up and they formed posses, hunted down alleged suspects, and hanged more than twenty men, all with no trials involved and often acting only upon vague accusations or rumors.

Sheriff Henry Plummer realized that the crowds of miners seeking revenge for the lost gold and lives of their fellows had gotten into a mob mentality. Justice no longer entered into their thinking nor their actions. They were out of control. Plummer knew it would be difficult, if possible at all, to stand up to the excited throng. He felt it his duty to stop the spree of hanging before it went any further. It certainly did not feel like the Christmas spirit had invaded the territory.

\* \* \*

*Friday, December 25, 1863. Christmas Day, Delavan, Wisconsin. After dinner at the Finn family residence.*

Maggie was miserable with the ill-effects of pregnancy, but at least Rob was home and being supportive of her in her condition. His gentle words and attentions went far to make her sufferings bearable. She believed she had nearly another month to wait for her first child to be born. Maggie was scared, a little, and nervous about the parts of childbirth that she knew little or nothing about. Rob assured her that Mrs. Rudd, the town mid-wife, could answer all her questions, and that the woman was competent to deliver and care for mother and child. His calm assurances helped Maggie some.

They'd talked about names. If the child was a boy, Rob wanted to honor his two lost sons by naming the child Michael Henry Finn. Margaret preferred the name Joseph for a boy-child and was as adamant about that as she was naming a girl-child Sarah. Rob acquiesced for the sake of keeping peace.

He wondered if his friend Henry Plummer had received his telegram wishing him Merry Christmas, and if Henry had yet left Bannack behind for Cedar Rapids. He hoped so.

John was riding Sadie around in a field behind the house. Lonnie watched the two work together. His practiced eye told him that the mare had wonderful lines for breeding and that John Finn was a natural horseman.

Patrick Murphy was enjoying dessert at the Adamses' table, having been invited to join them for Christmas Dinner. He and Jenna were seated side-by-side at the table, with Billy across from Patrick. Billy suspected it might not be too long before Patrick would go from being his friend to his brother-in-law. That thought made him happy.

Catherine Finn Duffy and her son, Tommy, enjoyed the early evening after a big dinner in Darien, hosted by Tommy's grandparents, Thomas and Ellen Duffy. As those in that role so often do, the elderly Duffys were already spoiling their grandson with presents and sweetmeats, all of which Catherine expected and allowed. She knew it was only for the few days of her visit, and did not want to deny her in-laws or her son the opportunity.

* * *

*Saturday, January 9th, 1864. In a teepee of a Sioux Indian village north of the Iowa-Minnesota border. Late afternoon.*

After adding fuel to the fire, Hotah's woman left the lodge, pulling the snug-fitting cover into the hatch opening behind her. Hotah looked across to his father, Mankato, who was visiting his son in celebration of the longer days.

"Tell me," said the older man in their native Dakota Siouxan tongue.

"It was right. There was justice. Inmutanka does not lie, does not choose wrong."

In his mind's eye, Hotah could see the lion edge its way out onto the tree limb.  He could feel the white man stiffen at the first touch of the big cat's paw to his throat, smell the man's fear as the claw was drawn three times across the neck.  When the cat turned to look at the other man still on horseback, he saw no enemy to attack, no quarry to devour.  Satisfied, the lion looked again into the dying white man's eyes, snarled and left.  It reached the edge of the ravine in a few leaps, stretching out before going over the edge.

Hotah's right hand stroked the stone-bladed knife sheathed on his hip.  Its sharp, jagged edge cut deeply, easily.  Its wound looked to some like the deep scratch of a lion's claw.

Mankato nodded to his remaining son.  There was justice, and it did not involve the white man's talk.

* * *

*Sunday, January 10, 1864.  As darkness settles onto Bannack City, Idaho Territory.*

Surprised by the intrusion into his quarters, Henry Plummer asked to speak with his sister-in-law (whom, along with her husband, he shared the cabin they'd bought from him) before being led out by the vigilantes who had come knocking minutes before.  They denied his request, so Henry called to Mrs. Vail over his shoulder, "Tell Electa

I'll see her in Iowa when this is over." Naturally, he expected he and his evidence would prevail at whatever trial this gang was planning.

Outside, in the street, two of his part-time deputies, Buck Stinson and Ned Ray, were already bound with their hands behind them. Henry Plummer was in the same condition moments later. All three men believed they were being taken someplace near to be tried for the accusations against them. They'd heard the rumors for almost a week. It puzzled them where the trial would be held, it being Sunday evening. Perhaps it would be held Monday morning, in which case they were probably going to the jail that Henry had built.

When Wilbur Sanders called out to his men, "head 'em to the gulch, boys," Plummer knew that no trial was intended. They were being marched to the gallows he had built this past summer.

"Wait just a minute, Sanders, there's no call for this." Henry Plummer fought hard to keep the quaver of fear from his voice. "What d'ya think you're doin'?"

Wilbur Sanders replied back confidently and loud enough for all in the vicinity to hear, including any bystanders in the dark, "We know exactly what we're doin' here, Plummer. We're carryin' out the sentence of the court that's found you all guilty of high crimes and murder. One of your gang confessed your guilt and there'll be no more of it!" Wilbur's voice rose in volume, pitch, and intensity as he shouted out the last phrase. He took a deep breath before continuing, "String 'em up, boys. Don't give 'em a drop–it's too good for 'em."

And so it happened that Sheriff Henry Plummer was convicted and executed without any trial or any defense, as were his two deputies. Similar fates attended all of the more than twenty-five men killed by the vigilante committee. No evidence, no defense, no records. Ironically, it was almost the same way the Federal government treated the Sioux Indians in Mankato, Minnesota twelve months plus two weeks earlier. And as unjust, though not as bloody, as the Bear River Massacre that same Federal government carried out eleven months prior.

Peace and justice were rare commodities in the States and Territories in 1863 and 1864, especially among commodities issued by governments.

\* \* \*

*Monday, January, 11, 1864. In an upstairs bedroom of the Finn house outside Delavan, Wisconsin.*

Maggie McDonald Finn winced and cried during the final hours of labor and birthing her first-born child. She did not scream. When she set her mind to something, Maggie could be absolutely stubborn in keeping to that goal. And she had told herself she would not scream.

All that pain and effort was over now, and she held her beautiful, perfect baby boy to her breast. He nuzzled and suckled comfortably while his mother now set her mind to enduring this process for the next eighteen months or so. Rob stood over the two of them, smiling a big, proud smile such as only fathers of newborns can do. Though he was handsome and she loved him, Maggie thought he looked dumb at that moment, like a big ape on the circus poster. She kept the thought to herself.

Part of Rob's joy came from the naming they'd finally agreed upon: Joseph Henry Finn. Rob's argument that the middle name would be for his good friend, Sheriff Henry Plummer, won the day.

He couldn't wait to send Plummer the telegram.

THE END

# End Notes

**Henry Plummer**, a genuine person from the history of this country, has a great deal of controversy attached to his life. He became the elected sheriff of both Bannack and Virginia City, which were booming gold mining towns. Those were rough-and-ready times with lots of robberies and killings taking place.

Henry didn't seem very effective in catching those responsible, some say that was because he was the leader of the outlaws. It is hard to know the facts at this late date; I was not there. The Federal government was involved behind the scenes and that often results in muddied waters. My take on Henry in this tale is different from what you'll find elsewhere. This work is fiction, but who knows?

---

The Sharps rifle that Longshot carries with him is quite a "shootin' iron". The company's products were known for their superior accuracy and durability. They are still prized among collectors for those traits and the role they played in history. The shooting feats described in the story are **extraordinary, not impossible.** Keep in mind that our hero is an extraordinary man. And by the way, the shot made in the opening paragraph IS possible, and I have the chronograph records to prove it. The black-powder-charged ball fired into a two mile per hour headwind, at

1,000 yards distance will have the projectile arriving a split-second **after** the sound.  And yes, it is a 'lobbed' shot.

---

    Many of the locations and routes that appear within the pages of the novel are real.  At a minimum, I attempt to keep my writing real by using the most accurate information and descriptions available to me.  Historical fiction should inform two groups of people: Writers and readers.  That's my story and I'm stickin' to it.

---

Thank you for reading my work.

Keith R. Baker  –  December 31, 2016
Ronan, Montana

External link(s) to maps, pictures and historical items of interest:

## www.KeithRBaker.com/longshot-links

## Other Books In This Series:

## LONGSHOT IN MISSOURI

## LONGSHOT INTO THE WEST

## BRIDGET'S STORY  (A short story prequel to the series)

# ABOUT THE AUTHOR

In addition to being an avid history and genealogy buff, Keith has been an avid outdoorsman his entire life. He has worn a variety of hats in the business world after completing two periods of duty with the US Navy. His hobbies apart from reading and research include shooting, teaching others the basics of gun safety & handling. Until recently he took an active role in local and regional politics as a public speaker and campaign consultant.

Keith and his wife Leni have enjoyed living several places in the US, including Illinois, Wisconsin, Missouri and Montana. They have two adult children, two adult foster children and nine grandchildren scattered around the country and the world.

Made in the USA
Middletown, DE
22 March 2017